# ACKNOWLEDGEMENTS

I'd like to extend a heartfelt thank you to the amazing members of the 'Psychological Thriller Readers' Facebook group. Your passion and discussions ignited the spark that led me to discover my true calling in the thriller/mystery genres. As an author, finding your niche can be a journey, and I'm grateful to this incredible community for guiding me to mine.

Home Sweet Hostage



Book Cover Design by bookcoverzone.com
Book Written by Jessica Lynn Sorensen
First Edition: June 2024

Published By:
Jessica Goldsney
Regina, SK

# Home Sweet Hostage

JESSICA LYNN SORENSEN

# PROLOGUE

## TWO YEARS BEFORE

The cool night air greeted me as I exited the restaurant, clutching the takeout bag filled with Chinese food. I remembered the extra shrimp this time. She will be happy.

Reaching my truck, I fumbled with my keys, eager to text my wife that I'd be home soon. Tonight, it was busy, and I was running a bit behind. Darn! I left my phone at the house. Sighing, I started the engine and pulled onto the road. It's less than a ten-minute drive. I'll be home soon.

Thoughts of my wife filled my mind as I drove. I had fallen in love with her all over again today. The look on her face zip lining was priceless. Kind of a turn on, actually. Lost in thought, I barely noticed the lights in my rearview mirror until they were right on my tail. A black SUV, its headlights glared through the darkness.

My heart raced, and an uneasy feeling crept in. I pressed down on the accelerator, hoping to outdistance the vehicle, but it surged forward, ramming into the side of my truck with a bone-jarring force. The impact sent me spinning off the highway, crashing hard into the ditch. My head slammed against the steering wheel, and everything went black.

I awoke to rough hands pulling me from the wreckage, my vision blurred and my head was throbbing. Two men loomed over me, their faces obscured by the darkness and the blood that trickled into my eyes. They barked questions at me, their voices harsh and demanding.

"Who are you?" one of them snarled.

Disoriented, I struggled to remember. "I... I don't know. What's happening? Where are you taking..."

They pushed me down into the dirt, their grip unyielding. "Who we are doesn't matter, Zyler. Who you are is what matters."

"Zyler," I repeated, the name sounding foreign on my

lips. Confusion clouded my mind as I tried to grasp my own identity.

My sight slipped away, the edges of my vision collapsing. Panic surged through me. I was powerless to stop it. The pain in my head intensified, throbbing with each heartbeat, and the taste of blood filled my mouth. My last conscious thought was a desperate plea for help, a silent scream in the night.

# CHAPTER 1

ZYLER

To hell with Jordana and her bullshit. That prick can have her. Such a Chad thing to do, moving in on another guy's girl. Soon, he will see the controlling person she truly is. Honestly, it seemed like I was living with Judge Judy.

I glanced at my new digs with excitement! Standing before the freshly painted door, about to step inside for the first time. Buying a house I have never stepped foot in was probably not the best idea.

*Okay!*

It was a terrible idea, but I did see a thorough virtual

view of the place, and it passed the home inspection. It did not occur to me that even home inspectors can *miss* things. Crucial things.

I inhaled deeper than ever before. *Smell that?* That is the smell of *freedom*. Moving into this place is like sticking a fork in the past and saying adios suckers! I am embracing the joys of singlehood. The *main* joy being that no one can cheat on me.

A lady opened the door, motioning for me to come in. She must be the realtor. She is here to wrap up the finishing touches on the sale.

*Wow!* She is kinda hot for a redhead. She has that sexy librarian vibe.

*Wonder if she is single?* Not wanting a relationship, but open to playing the field for a while.

As I step inside, the rooms appear as if they are eagerly waiting to be bombarded with my useless shit. I can already picture myself chilling in the comfy living room, whipping up some magic in the kitchen, and treating some lucky ladies to my bedroom.

*Perfect!*

The realtor is a chatty lady, following me like a shadow, waiting to handle any questions I throw her way.

The décor is strange. Not my style, but it'll work for now.

"So, lemme get this straight. All this stuff came with the house, right?" I quipped, shooting a sly grin at the realtor as I took in the odd-looking furniture.

"Yep, you got it," she remarked with a little head bob. "You get the whole shebang, furniture and all!"

I smiled at the idea of scoring everything inside the crib. "That's awesome," I exclaimed. "My ex snagged all our stuff, and honestly, I couldn't be bothered to fight her for it. That's why I moved. I can't even stand to be in the same state as her cheating a..." I stopped myself. No need to give her the entire story.

She let out a little chuckle. It sounded like a *pity* one. "Well, glad we could rescue you from your predicament!"

"I'm glad you called me when you saw my ad," I stated. "This place is just what I was looking for."

"What can I say? I recognize a good fit when I see one. I have a feeling you will fit in more than you realize," she said in a friendly yet sinister tone.

Why would she say it like that?

"I guess we will see," I replied.

She started rambling on about all the fancy features and perks, throwing in some neighborhood gossip to spice things up. She mentioned the last girl kicked the bucket, and this house was an estate sale.

*Now I get why it was so cheap.*

It was sad to hear a young lady died, but it made my life easier.

As I wandered through the rooms of my new place, my eyes swept over the pictures on the walls. There was something peculiar about them, something that made me pause and examine them closely.

*This girl liked some weird shit.*

"Well, it looks like everything is in order," she said, turning to face me. "It's all yours."

I nodded, experiencing a surge of excitement. "Thanks so much for all your help throughout this process," I replied. "I appreciate it."

"It was my pleasure," the realtor affirmed with a smile. "I'm just glad we were able to find you the *perfect* place."

I smiled, experiencing a sense of gratitude wash over me. "I can't wait to make it my own," I said. "I've got big plans for this place."

The realtor laughed under her breath. "I'm sure you'll

do wonders with it. You moved in, just in time," she mumbled.

As she turned to leave, I felt uneasy. "Thanks again," I said, stepping forward to shake her hand. "I couldn't have done this without you."

"Anytime," she replied. "Don't hesitate to reach out if you ever need anything."

With a wave, the realtor headed out the door, leaving me standing in the doorway of my new home. I glanced around the place. My heart raced with excitement.

*Hell yeah!*

*Home sweet home!*

I made my way outside to the backyard. The sight that greeted me was nothing short of breathtaking. The sun was shining down on the grass and flowers. A beautiful creek flowed peacefully behind the house, its waters cascading over some rocks.

As I gazed up at the sky, a plane flew overhead, its contrail streaking across the blue sky. I smiled, experiencing a sense of contentment descending upon me. I looked back at the house.

*This is all mine.*

My phone buzzed in my pocket. I pulled it out to see

a message from Stacy. My heart sank as I read her words:

> HEY, I CAN'T MAKE OUR DATE TONIGHT. SOMETHING CAME UP. CAN WE MAKE IT ON FRIDAY INSTEAD?

"Well, that sucks," I mumbled into the air. I had been looking forward to seeing her. She's the only person I know here. With a resigned sigh, I texted back.

> NO PROB, STACE. SEE YOU FRIDAY!

I slipped my phone back into my pocket and turned my attention back to the house. Since it was getting late, I left unloading the truck for the morning.

As I stepped back into the house, my eyes fell upon a framed photograph on one of the end tables. In the picture, a smiling girl stood arm in arm with a guy. *That must be her.* She looked so vibrant, so full of life.

*Wonder what happened to her?*

Another brunette, I noted silently, my mind drifting to the brunettes I had known in the past. An image of Jordana sleeping with Chad tasered my mind.

*Done with brunettes. I'm sticking with blondes or gingers from now on.*

I stood in the bedroom, and a wave of unease washed

over me as I glanced at the bed. It was an odd sensation, almost like an invasion, to be lying in someone else's bed. The sheets and pillows probably still carry her lingering scent.

*Screw that!*

I stripped down to my boxers and grabbed a spare blanket from the closet, spreading it out on the floor beside the bed. It wasn't the most comfortable setup, but it would have to do for tonight. Better than sleeping in her bed.

*Tomorrow, I'm buying my own bed and tossing that old thing out.*

# CHAPTER 2

As I groggily blinked my eyes open, feeling disoriented and achy, a jolt of pain zapped through my entire being as I tried to stretch out. That's getting older for ya. The thing you do to prevent pulled muscles ends up pulling your damn muscles. The floor was a bad idea.

As I stood up, I glanced over and saw her—a random chick sleeping in my bed.

*What the fuck?*

There is a lady in my bed. I stared at her with my mouth open.

*How the hell did she get in here? When?*

I rubbed my eyes, trying to shake reality into them. No

way! I'm seeing things.

She moved.

I quickly tiptoed out of the room. Pacing in the hall-way, I tried to plan my next move.

What does someone do when they wake up their first morning in their new home, and a stranger is sprawled out in their bed?

I put my hands on my head. *Think, man! I know. Just wake her up and ask her why she is in my house.*

*I got this!*

I peeked into the room. She rolled over, and I quickly hid behind the door. With a wave of bravery mixed with curiosity, I walked to the side of the bed.

*Wow!*

Her brown hair looks like a dirty tornado hit her head and landed on my pillow! Not a quiet sleeper. That's for sure. Snores like a bear. She smells like whiskey. Bet she had a rough night.

Pushing her arm, I said, "Um... ma'am."

Her eyes widened in shock, as if she had just seen a ghost. Her voice trembled as she whispered my name.

"Zyler?" A tear slid down her cheek. "I thought you were dead," she cried out.

*Dead?* I looked at her, trying to place where I might have seen her before. "Have we met before?" I asked cautiously.

She shook her head. Her sobs made it difficult for her to speak clearly. "I can't believe you're alive." She reached out to hug me.

Instinctively, I recoiled, pulling away from her. "Why are you in my bed?" I demanded, looking around the room. "How did you get in here?"

Her eyes widened in confusion. Tears streamed down her face. "This is my bed," she replied, her voice quivering. "Our bed, actually." Her words sent a shiver down my spine. I looked around, trying to make sense of this bizarre situation. She reached out and gently took my hand. Her gaze fixated on my finger, and a gasp escaped her lips. "Where's your ring?" she whispered.

I looked down at my hand. "What ring?"

"Your wedding ring," she replied, her eyes pleading with me to understand.

*My wedding ring?* What the hell is happening right now? Panic clawed at my chest. "I don't..." I stuttered. "I have never been married. Why would I have a ring?"

Shit! I made her cry again.

"You don't remember?" she repeated, her gaze searching mine for a flicker of recognition. "You don't remember me? Us?"

The room spun around me. I swallowed the lump that formed in my throat. Perhaps it was my soul trying to run from this moment. "I'm sorry," I croaked out. "I don't know who you are. I have never seen you before."

She looked at me with a mixture of heartbreak and longing, her hands trembling as she reached out to touch my face. "We were supposed to grow old together, Zyler?" She cried harder. "I tried to find you," she confessed between the sobs. "After you disappeared."

"Disappeared?" I blurted out. "I don't know what the hell you are talking about. I have lived in the same place my entire life until yesterday. I bought this house. This is my house."

She stared at me, confused as all hell. "This is our house, Zyler. Actually, it is *my* house now. You took off for two years without a trace. Never bothered to reach out to me or anything."

What the hell is she on?

"Are you still drunk?" I laughed at the absurdity of the situation.

"Is this funny to you? Do you know how long I have grieved you? How many nights I cried myself to sleep thinking my husband was dead?"

"No, I don't. But I *know* I'm not your husband. I don't know how you know my first name. Good guess."

She bolted out of the bed, walked up to me, and looked me dead in the face. "Yeah, because *Zyler Dixon* is such a common name," she mocked in a frustrated tone.

My mouth fell open like the Grand Canyon. *I can't believe this girl.* Jordana had to put her up to this.

"Did Jordana pay you to screw with me or something?"

Her confusion grew. "Who is Jordana?" Her eyes widened as she spoke, and another tear strolled down her cheek. "Is that the girl you left me for?" she mumbled through gritted teeth.

"What? No. Jordana is my ex. The reason I moved here was to start over in the first place." *Oh, great!* Now she looked even more pissed.

"I can't believe you right now. You go missing for two years, then show up and pretend we were never married. Then you have the audacity to throw the woman you left me for in my face. How dare you?"

This has to be a nightmare. *Wake up!* I pinched myself. Nope! Felt that.

"Listen lady, I have never met you in my life. I don't know what you are talking about. But you need to leave."

"No!" she shouted. "You need to leave."

"This is my house. I'm not going anywhere." I grabbed the documents showing I bought the house and shoved them in her face. "See... as of yesterday, this house is mine. Vanessa Marsh's estate sold it to me."

"I don't know where you got this fraudulent paper," she snapped, snatching the document from my hand. She shook it angrily. "I did not sell my house."

That's when it clicked. *She's the woman in the pictures.* I hadn't recognized her because she looked different—probably all done up, maybe filtered. I inhaled deeply, my head spinning. "This doesn't make any sense. Are you... Vanessa?" I asked, pointing to her.

"Obviously!" she exclaimed.

I shook my head in disbelief. "That isn't possible. Vanessa Marsh is *dead.*"

# CHAPTER 3

## VANESSA

**EIGHT YEARS AGO**

I sat there, anxiously waiting for my date to arrive, sipping on my coffee. He said he would be here twenty minutes ago. Unless he's a ghost, he lied. *I hate dating.* I don't even know why I bother anymore. Between the no-shows, the players, the cheaters, the ones that only want a hookup, and the ones that plan your future together in the first ten minutes, it's all just a waste of time. The older I get, the more appealing becoming a cat lady looks.

I glanced at my phone again to see if I had missed an explanatory message. *Nothing!* I scoffed to myself. *This is embarrassing.* Inhaling deeply, I leaned back in my chair. The chair, creaky and worn, decided it had enough of supporting my weight—and all my emotional baggage. With a loud crack, it gave way beneath me, and I fell on my ass.

I heard gasps and snickers from the other patrons as I lay sprawled on the floor, my face burning with embarrassment. *Okay! This is more humiliating.* And then, in the midst of my humiliation, he appeared.

"Are you okay?" he asked, trying not to laugh.

*Oh my God! A total hottie just saw me break a chair with my ass. I wonder if he has a gun so I can shoot myself.*

I groaned, a mix of pain and embarrassment spiraling through me. "Physically or mentally?" I replied, trying to salvage what little dignity I had left.

He chuckled. "Um, both, I guess?" he quipped with a smile, extending a hand to help me up.

I grabbed his hand, and he helped me to my feet. A small dimple appeared on his cheek when he smiled. I felt a rush of butterflies in my stomach—the kind you get when your crush acknowledges your existence at school.

Once I was standing, he continued to check if I was truly okay. His genuine concern and calm demeanor helped ease my embarrassment. *This guy is so worried about me, yet Karl didn't even bother to show up.*

"So, is the coffee so bad that you destroyed their chair?" he teased.

I turned even redder. I tried to talk, but nothing came out.

He reached out to shake my hand. "Name's Zyler."

"Well then, tell me, Zyler, how many times are you going to try to hold my hand today?"

He laughed. "The first time doesn't count. I was just picking you up," he said, laughing even harder when he realized how it sounded.

I felt a blush creep up my cheeks. "Good thing I was stood up by the other dude then," I confessed with a nervous chuckle.

"His loss. What's the name of that pretty face of yours?"

"Vanessa," I introduced myself.

"Vanessa," Zyler repeated my name, savoring the sound on his lips. "A beautiful name for a beautiful woman." His words made me blush. Again!

Before I could respond, Zyler leaned back in his chair, a playful grin tugging at the corners of his lips. "So, Vanessa, now that I know your name, would you mind sharing a more personal detail with me? Perhaps your number?" he inquired.

His boldness made me laugh, and I couldn't deny the attraction that pulsed between us. I reached for a napkin on the table and scribbled my number down, sliding it across to him with a mischievous gleam in my eyes. "I suppose it's only fair for rescuing me off the floor," I teased.

Zyler's grin widened as he pocketed the napkin. "Who knew picking you up would lead to *picking you up*?" he punctuated his cheesy line with a wink.

"Are you hijacking my date?" I teased.

"Are you saying we are now on a date?"

"NO!" I exclaimed, slightly embarrassed. *Don't scare the guy away before he even has a chance to call.*

"That guy is an ass. One day, he'll regret not showing up, because you seem pretty awesome to me."

I blushed. "Typical birthday for me. I should have known he'd be a ghoster. My birthdays never go as planned."

"No way! It's your actual birthday today?"

"Yup," I shrugged.

He grinned. "It was my birthday yesterday."

"Well then... I guess I should say happy birthday to *us*," I replied.

"Guess our birthday gift from the universe was for us to meet."

I smiled. A guy had never been this nice to me before. Sure, guys have been nice—to burrow their way into my pleasure tunnel. But Zyler seemed different. He appeared to actually be interested in my feelings.

He stood up and extended his hand again. I looked at it, raising a questioning eyebrow.

"What do you say we get out of here and go to a matinee movie for your birthday? The prick left you hanging, and I can't leave without knowing you're going to have a good day," he proposed.

"I'm sure you *can* leave. I'm just a stranger in the coffee shop. You'll forget all about me in a week."

"Nope. I'm too invested now. Come on! Are you just going to leave me hanging with my hand out, or what?" he persisted.

I laughed and let him pull me up, dusting off my pants again. "Fine! But I get to pick the movie."

"Of course," he replied.

"Normally, I like suspense and horror movies, but today I'm feeling like a sappy romance chick flick," I admitted.

He gave me a side-eye with a half-grin. "I see how it is."

Little did I know that a simple coffee shop disaster would lead to my future husband. Maybe my chair was struck with Cupid's arrow.

# CHAPTER 4

## ZYLER

It had been surprisingly quiet since I came out of the bathroom. *Where did she go?* Maybe she was a ghost. The only plausible explanations were that this was a nightmare, or she really *was* a ghost. Perhaps Jordana had driven me to the brink of sanity, and now I was seeing things.

She got upset when I told her I couldn't listen to any more of her nonsense. I can't deal with crazy before coffee, especially when it involves supposedly dead people. I needed to get ready and buy a new bed.

I pushed the door open in a rush. *Holy shit! You've*

*got to be kidding me.* Her wrist was handcuffed to the metal leg of the bed. I'm pretty sure my jaw hit the floor.

"What on earth are you doing?"

Vanessa's gaze met mine. "I'm not leaving," she declared. "You can't make me."

My heart pounded in my chest. *Yup! This chick is a nutcase.*

"Girl, this is insane," I protested, trying to keep my voice steady. "You can't just handcuff yourself to the bed."

She shrugged, a hint of defiance flashing in her eyes. "Looks like I already did," she retorted, daring me to challenge her further.

A surge of frustration and anger welled up inside me, so intense I couldn't even find the right words. I grabbed my phone.

"If you call the cops, I'll tell them *you* did this," she warned, gesturing to the handcuffs.

Well, for fuck's sake.

I stared at her, my face tense with frustration and disbelief. "You're seriously going to hold yourself hostage in my house?"

Vanessa scoffed, her eyes flashing with annoyance.

"Well, technically, I'm holding myself hostage," she countered, her voice rising with defiance, "in *our* house."

I shook my head in disbelief. *How the hell did we get here?* "You're freaking crazy," I mumbled under my breath, unable to suppress the irritation bubbling to the surface.

But Vanessa wasn't backing down. "No, babe, *you* are!" she spat, her voice dripping with frustration. "I wouldn't have to do this if you'd just let me show you our life together."

I clenched my fists at my sides. *This girl is an effing whack job.* Yet, as I looked into her eyes, there was something deeper there—a flicker of pain and longing. As lost as she seemed, maybe she was just as confused as I was.

Inhaling deeply, I tried to calm the whirlwind of emotions inside me. "Vanessa, for god's sake!" I snapped. "Stop the act. We need to discuss this house situation. There's obviously been some kind of mistake."

"What act?" she asked, her tone sharpening.

"Pretending I'm your husband."

"It's not an act, Zyler. Let me prove it to you. Think of my birthday."

I threw my hands up in frustration. "I don't even *remember* you. How the hell am I supposed to remember your damn birthday?"

Her eyes filled with tears again, threatening to spill over. "It's the day after yours. We always joked that we were each other's gifts from the universe."

My eyes widened. *What?* "Huh? Alrighty then..." She couldn't have possibly known that. I let out an enormous sigh. "When's your birthday, then?"

"August 20th."

I couldn't help but laugh, convinced she had snooped through my wallet. "I see you went through my wallet."

"I didn't! I swear, I don't even know where your wallet is."

Speaking of my wallet, where the hell *was* it? I glanced over at the floor where I passed out last night. There it was, chillin' under the bed like it was hiding from this psycho. Even my wallet was scared of her. I snatched it up, keeping my eyes locked on her the entire time.

This chick is obviously stalking me. I scratched my head to think. *Oh wow! I need a shower. Worst dandruff ever.*

A loud knock at the door made us both jump. "Who

is that?" I squealed.

"How should I know? My phone is over there. I'm handcuffed to the bed, in case you forgot?" she growled, waving her hand around.

Well, this looks bad as all hell. I walked out of the room and peeked out the window. Who's that guy? He looks familiar. I looked at the picture on the end table. "Oh no," I whispered to myself. *It's him. Great! It looks like I'm keeping her against her will.*

I swung open the door and gave him a look over. He stared at me like I've got four eyes or a freaking horn sprouting out of my head. "Hi, ahh... I think I have the wrong house," he blurted with a shaky voice, bolting to his car.

# CHAPTER 5

## VANESSA

**SEVEN YEARS AGO**

The hospital room was quiet. The only sound was the soft beep of the monitors and the faint rustle of bed sheets. Zyler and I stood side by side, our hands clasped tightly as we visited my mom. Her battle with cancer had taken its toll, and now she lay in a hospital bed, her strength waning with each passing moment. She fought so hard, but that's the thing with cancer... it has no mercy.

I glanced over at Zyler, gratitude welling up inside me

for his unwavering support. My dad couldn't make it here today, but Zyler had insisted on being there for me.

My mom's eyes fluttered open as she turned to us with a weak smile. "Thank you for being here," she whispered.

Zyler squeezed my hand in response. "Of course, Mom," I replied, my voice choked with emotion.

She reached out, taking Zyler's hand in hers with surprising strength. Leaning in close, she whispered something in his ear, her words a private exchange between them. Then, turning to both of us, she spoke with a quiet determination.

"You two are going to do great things," she said, her voice filled with conviction. "You're the perfect couple, and even though I'll be leaving this world soon, I'll never leave your hearts."

My eyes turned from a mist to a waterfall. I tried to be strong for her. I really did. For the year she was sick, I succeeded. But this moment was different. I could feel her slipping away. I knew one of the worst moments in my life was soon to come. How do I live in this world without the woman who brought me into it? I prayed for a miracle every day she has been sick. No changes! Today, I'm begging for one. Please, let my mom be able to see her daughters get married.

"I'm so proud of you, Vanessa," my mom continued. "And Zyler, I'm proud of the man you are and the way you treat my daughter with such love and respect."

We all started crying.

When we left that day, I hugged my mom longer than usual. I sensed it would be the last time she'd hug me back.

Two days later, my mom passed away, leaving a hole in my heart that could never be filled. It was one of the hardest moments of my life, a loss that changed me in ways I never could have imagined. The only person who kept me going, the one who got me through it, was Zyler.

A month later, we went to visit my mom's grave. We had made a promise to visit her every month for the first year. The crisp autumn air wrapped around us as we wandered through the graveyard, the sun painting streaks of gold across the sky. It was the perfect day to visit her.

I walked up to her headstone and rubbed my hand along the top. I noticed Zyler wasn't beside me. I turned back to see him on one knee.

*Oh my god! Is he doing what I think he is?* I gasped in delight, hardly able to believe my eyes. "Babe, what are you doing?" I asked, my heart about to leap out of my chest.

He grinned. "I wanted to do something special," he explained, his voice filled with warmth. "Something that was as unique and beautiful as you are."

Well, proposing in a graveyard is definitely unique.

With trembling hands, Zyler reached for the note, his eyes never leaving mine as he began to read. "My dearest love," he began, his voice steady but filled with emotion. "From the moment I met you, I knew you were someone special. You bring light into my life in ways I..." He suddenly threw the note to the ground. "Screw that. Vanessa, during our last visit with your mom, she whispered to me that her final wish was for me to become her son-in-law. She said I was meant for you, that we have a love she never believed was possible, and she felt blessed to have seen it with her own eyes."

Tears rolled down my face as I listened to his words.

"And so," he continued, his voice shaking, "I wanted to share this moment with your mom." He reached into his pocket and pulled out a small velvet box, opening it to reveal the most gorgeous ring I had ever seen.

"Vanessa, will you make me the luckiest man in the world for being my wife? Will you marry me?" he asked, as a tear slid down his cheek.

A lump formed in my throat as I gazed down at him, overwhelmed by the depth of his love. "Yes, babe," I exclaimed, kneeling down into his arms.

He gently placed the ring on my finger, and as I admired its sparkling brilliance, we rose to our feet. He pulled me into his arms and gave me a tight squeeze, both of our faces a soppy mess.

After a moment of shared silence, we walked hand in hand to my mom's headstone. Standing together, we captured a photograph, the ring gleaming on my finger as we smiled for the camera.

With a sense of bittersweet joy, we shared the image on social media, accompanied by a heartfelt caption: "She said yes, with her mom by her side."

# CHAPTER 6

## ZYLER

I need to get out of here. I couldn't go back into the bedroom. What if she never leaves? I've poured all my hard-earned money into this house. This can't really be happening.

As I paced back and forth in the hallway, my mind raced with dark thoughts. *I could kill her. She's already dead. Maybe this time she will cross over. What am I thinking? I can't kill her.*

I took a deep breath, preparing myself for what I had to do. *Here goes nothing.* I pushed open the door to the bedroom. She looked up at me. She hasn't even moved. *Maybe she is the devil.* I know of the song, but I didn't think the devil was actually in Georgia. Why did I pick this state? I shook my head. *Should have gone to California.*

"Uncuff yourself and leave," I said, my voice cold and firm. I watched as her eyes widened in surprise, a flicker of uncertainty crossing her face.

"Not happening," she spat back, her words laced with venom.

"A guy showed up at the door, looked at me strange, and then took off. I don't know what is happening, but it needs to stop."

"Warren," she said under her breath. "Sorry. I know it must be hard to picture me with another guy. I thought you were dead, Zyler. I had to move on."

I put my hand on my forehead and clenched my jaw. "What? No. I don't care who you sleep with. We are not married," I yelled, feeling a surge of frustration rising within me. I tried reasoning with her. *There's only one way to end this gong show.* "Fine," I said. "Since you won't leave, I'm calling the cops."

I turned on my heel, striding out of the room to retrieve my phone. I dialed the emergency number, my heart pounding in my chest as I waited for someone to answer on the other end.

"This is an emergency. I need your help," I said with a quivering voice.

The dispatcher on the other end listened as I explained the situation—the handcuffs, the refusal to leave. But as I spoke, I could sense a shift in the tone of the conversation, a growing sense of disbelief in the dispatcher's voice.

"Let me get this straight. You have a woman in your house that has handcuffed herself to your bed?" the dispatcher asked, her words dripping with sarcasm.

"Correct."

"So, a woman is holding herself hostage in your house?"

"Yes! Against my will, might I add."

"I'm sorry, sir. I get that some kind of weird bedroom fetish thing turned into a hot mess, but we have more important matters to deal with."

"No, no bedroom thing. I've never seen this woman before today. She won't get out of my house." I tried to reason with the dispatcher, to make her see that this was not what it sounded like. But her tone remained dismissive.

*Screw this!* I hung up the phone. A sense of defeat washed over me. I had pinned my hopes on the authorities to help me resolve this nightmare, but now it seemed that even they wanted nothing to do with this woman.

I went back into the bedroom. I took a step closer to her, my gaze unwavering. "Why are you doing this?" I asked, my voice tinged with desperation.

Her eyes met mine, the mask of defiance slipping away to reveal a flicker of regret. "I'm sorry," she whispered.

At that moment, I discerned a flicker of fear in her eyes—fear mirroring my unease. I realized then that she was just as uncomfortable and apprehensive as I was. I needed her to open up, to reveal more.

"Show me," I urged, my voice gentle yet firm.

She lifted her gaze to meet mine, her expression guarded. "Show you what?" she inquired.

"Take the handcuffs off and show me... us," I clarified, my heart pounding with anticipation. "Show me any proof you have. Pictures, videos, anything." Doubt gnawed at me, but the prospect of uncovering the truth compelled me forward. It might be the only way to convince her to leave.

A mixture of sadness and relief washed over her features. "I will. Thank you," she responded in a shaky voice. She took off the handcuffs and disappeared into the spare room. Moments later, she returned clutching a photo album, settling onto the bed beside me.

As she opened the album, she stated, "This is our wedding album." I drew in a deep breath, summoning the strength to confront whatever was to come. My gaze fell upon the photographs, and my heart skipped a beat. Nothing could have prepared me for what I was about to see.

She pointed at the pictures, looked at me, and said, "See, I wasn't lying."

*No freaking way! This can't be real.* I looked down to see dozens of wedding pictures—pictures of this girl marrying me.

# CHAPTER 7

## VANESSA

**SIX YEARS AGO**

My hands trembled slightly as I smoothed down the delicate fabric of my beautiful wedding dress. *He is going to love it.*

I glanced over at my dad. His eyes were misty with emotion as he looked at me—his little girl, all grown up and about to get married. He reached out and grabbed my hand.

"You look stunning, sweetheart," he whispered. "Your mother would be so proud of you."

Tears welled up in my eyes as I hugged him, feeling a rush of gratitude for the man who had raised me. My dad is the best father I could have ever been blessed with.

As we shared a moment of quiet reflection, my maid of honor leaned in with a grin to lighten the mood.

"You know, there's still time to make a run for it," she teased.

I laughed, shaking my head in mock exasperation. "Not a chance," I countered. "I'll never find anyone as special as Zyler."

And just like that, the music began to play. *Oh, lord... it's time.* With a deep breath, I took my dad's arm, and together we stepped out into the aisle.

As I walked down the aisle, everyone's gaze shifted towards me. My eyes were locked on the man waiting for me at the end. There he was. My heart skipped a beat as I caught sight of him. He looked so handsome. A lump formed in my throat as I fought back tears, not wanting to ruin my makeup before the ceremony even began.

At that moment, all my fears and uncertainties melted away. This was it—the moment I had been waiting for, the moment I would become Vanessa Dixon in front of our family and friends. With each step closer to him, a wave of gratitude swept through me. As I reached the end of the aisle, I reached out to take Zyler's hand in mine.

Moments later, the time had come to exchange our vows. We turned to face each other, and I held his hands in mine, feeling the warmth and reassurance in his grip.

I grinned. "Well, babe, here we are."

He smirked. "Here we are. Do you remember that one day after the sappy romance movie you made me watch, when I said one day that will be us?"

I laughed. "Yes."

"Do you remember what you said?"

I glanced over at all the faces in the room, then turned back to look directly into his eyes. "I said... don't count on it."

He squeezed my hands. "That's the thing, babe. I never counted on it. I knew! From the moment I saw you crash on the floor in the coffee shop, I fell right along with you."

I blushed. A single tear rolled down my face. "Who knew that getting ghosted would become the best thing that ever happened to me?"

He smiled. "I vow to never leave the toilet seat up unless it's payback for something."

"I promise to always make room for your favorite snacks in the pantry, even if it means giving up some of mine," I vowed, my voice full of warmth.

"Vanessa, I promise to be your partner in crime, your partner in Netflix binges, and even your partner in those overly dramatic dance routines you love so much," he added, his eyes sparkling with mischief and love.

*So embarrassing.* I can't believe he brought up the dancing. "I promise to listen to your rants about video game characters like they're real people."

He chuckled and let out a pretend, offended scoff. "I promise to always be your confidante, your shoulder to lean on, and your partner in tackling all the challenges life throws our way, especially the ones involving spiders."

"Zyler, as we take this step forward together, I vow to be your rock when the storms come."

"I pick you, Vanessa, today, tomorrow, and forever. My love for you surpasses everything else, and I will dedicate my life to showing you just how much you mean to me!"

"I pick you too, babe," I declared, my voice filled with warmth and affection. "And I can't wait to spend the rest of our lives together, making each other laugh, rolling our eyes, and cherishing all those little moments that define us."

After we finished, the pastor took over.

"As you embark on this new chapter of your lives together, may you always cherish the bond you share, and may your love for one another grow stronger with each passing day."

With a final blessing, he concluded the ceremony.

"Ladies and gentlemen, it is my pleasure to present to you for the first time, Mr. and Mrs. Zyler and Vanessa Dixon."

# CHAPTER 8

## ZYLER

I stared at the photographs spread out before me, disbelief knotting my stomach. Pictures of me, or someone who looked exactly like me, in situations I have never been in. Kissing a woman I've never kissed, posing with a bunch of dudes I've never seen before, and smiling alongside individuals who I am assuming are this guy's parents.

"This can't be me," I mumbled, unable to reconcile the images with my reality. "I mean, look at that haircut. I'd never..."

"Zyler, that's you," she interrupted, pointing to a picture of me near the wedding cake.

I shook my head vigorously. "That's not me. It's some doppelgänger with weird ass hair."

She shot me a look that implied she thought I'd lost my mind, and honestly, I was starting to wonder myself. This was like some bizarre fever dream; worse than any drug-induced hallucination I'd experienced back in college. And trust me, that's saying something—I never touched drugs again after that.

"I'm showing you proof, and you're still denying it?" she exclaimed. "Was I that terrible of a wife?"

"First, I wouldn't know," I retorted, frustration bubbling up inside me. "And I'm not lying. It's some guy that looks like me. Everyone has someone in the world that resembles them."

"Looks like you?" She let out a wild laugh. "Looks like you?" she shouted. "With the same name, birthday, and also born in Nevada. Do you hear how crazy that sounds?"

"How do you even know where I was born?" I demanded, feeling a chill creep down my spine.

She looked at me with a *you can't be serious* face.

I let out a mix of a laugh with a deep inhale. "I get it

now. You are a stalker. How long have you been stalking me?"

She let out an offended noise. "You are so delusional right now."

"Look in the mirror, lady."

She scoffed.

We sat in tense silence for a moment before I snapped. "That's it. I want a husband test."

"A what?" she asked, eyebrows creasing in confusion.

"A test, but for husbands," I clarified, gesturing wildly. "To prove..."

"DNA?" she interrupted.

"Yes!" I exclaimed. "I want a damn DNA test, and when it comes back negative, I'll shove it in your face."

"More like look like a fool with a positive result," she retorted.

"Whatever!" I spat, feeling the tension crackling between us.

"Yeah, whatever! Do it!" she snarled.

"I will... as soon as I figure out how. Feel free to leave until the results come in. Go stay at Mr. Runaway's place."

"I can't."

"Why not? You two look happy in that picture."

"He doesn't want to see me right now because he thinks my husband rose from the dead, and I'm back with him," she explained, her voice tinged with frustration.

"Bring him over. I can tell him that is definitely not the case. You aren't even my type," I suggested, trying to inject some lightness into the tense situation.

*Really?* I made her cry again. "Sorry, I didn't mean..." I began, but she waved me off. Clearly, she was not in the mood for apologies.

I sighed, feeling defeated. *I give up! Screw this!* "O kay... this has been a fun conversation and all, but I'm going to town to grab a few things." Like a huge bottle of vodka. "I need a break from all of this," I added, motioning my hand around the room before landing a pointed gesture at her.

Snatching my keys off the table, I marched toward the door. It closed behind me with more force than I intended. I stepped outside, and the wind whipped through my clothes. This has been the longest day of my life. That lady needs to be in a psych ward or something.

As I drove onto the highway, I seriously pondered

whether I should return. I adore the house. Ideal for me. But a wife was not supposed to be a part of the package. Guess that's why they say to read the fine print before signing.

I turned on the radio... *Every Breath You Take* was playing. "Oh, come on," I shouted. I switched the station. *Your House*—Alanis Morrisette was on the next station. "I see how it is," I grunted to the air. *To hell with music,* I thought, flicking it off.

The drive to Pooler was only five minutes. I pulled up to the liquor store. As I made my way toward the entrance, people were giving me odd looks, their eyes lingering on me a little too long for comfort.

Ignoring their stares, I hurried inside. I beelined for the vodka aisle, snatching a bottle and some mix. Just as I turned to leave, I rammed into someone. My truck keys slipped from my grasp and clattered to the floor. As I bent to retrieve them, I glanced up to see who I'd collided with. A man's eyes widened in recognition, causing him to stagger backwards and almost choke on his own breath.

"Dixon?"

# CHAPTER 9

"Hey, sorry, do I know you?" I asked, trying to place where I might have seen him before.

"It's me, Glenn! From high school."

I racked my brain, trying to remember a Glenn from my school days. But I couldn't place him at all. "Glenn... I'm sorry, but I don't think we went to the same high school. My last name is Dixon, though," I replied, hoping it would clear up any confusion.

Glenn's smile faltered for a moment before he let out a loud laugh. "Oh man, you're pulling my leg! I know it's you. You haven't changed at all. Remember our old crew, hanging out by the bleachers during lunch breaks?"

I couldn't help but chuckle at his persistence. "I'm sorry, Glenn. I really don't remember you."

"Does Dennis know you are back?"

"Dennis, who?"

He gave a sarcastic sigh. "Your dad. I saw him a month ago, and he mentioned you have been missing for a couple of years. He thought..."

"Let me guess... he thought I was dead," I interrupted.

"Yeah," he whispered.

*Guess Vanessa isn't the only one losing it in this place. My actual father died 6 years ago. Around the time I supposedly got married without knowing it.*

"Hey man, it was nice seeing you," I said to shut him up, then continued, "but I need to get going."

"No problem. We should catch up sometime."

*Dude! I'm not who you think. Get that in your head.*
"For sure."

As I walked out the door, a lady yelled, "Nice of you finally to come home to your wife."

"Whatever, lady," I shouted, hopping in my truck. I revved the engine and peeled out of the parking lot. *This place is fucked. I should have stayed in Nevada.*

It's like I'm trapped in a never-ending nightmare, with

everything spiraling further out of control. I can't believe this is actually happening to me. There's no guidebook for a situation like this. This is definitely not the fresh start I was expecting. You'd think Stacy would have mentioned there's a missing person around here who looks exactly like me and has my name. *Actually, I should call her ass.*

"Hey Zy, how are you liking it here?"

"Stace, why didn't you tell me there's a missing person who looks like me with my name?"

Stacy's silence on the matter fueled my annoyance further. As I awaited her response, my mind raced with a flurry of emotions. Thoughts of confusion, suspicion, and frustration swirled in my head.

"What are you talking about?"

"The guy that's missing. Everyone keeps mistaking me for him."

"Are you serious?"

"No... I just picked up a new way to flirt with you. Yes! I'm serious. Oh, and it gets better. Did you know I'm married?"

She laughed. "Didn't know you were married, Zyler."

"I'm not! But according to the woman that refuses to

*leave* my house, I'm her husband."

"Well, that sounds like quite the pickle you've found yourself in, Zy," she replied. "I hope you have a good divorce lawyer on speed dial," she teased.

"This isn't funny, Stacy."

"Are you drunk?"

I groaned in frustration. "No, I'm not. Why would you think that?"

"Because you sound ridiculous right now."

"Thanks, Stace. Forget it. I figured you would be a little more supportive, since you were the one who convinced me to move here."

"I'm sorry! I swear I didn't know anything about a missing person. I'll check it out when I get home."

"Thank you."

"I gotta go. I'll call ya later," she asserted, quickly hanging up the phone.

I whipped off my hat and ruffled my fingers through my hair. It struck me as strange how everyone automatically assumes I'm this missing guy, while the one person I actually know here seems completely unaware of the situation.

# CHAPTER 10

## STACY

### 18 MONTHS AGO

The car rumbled to a stop as my boss pointed out the window, his gaze fixed on a man roaming through the farmer's market. "You see that guy? That's Zyler Dixon," he said, his voice low and serious. "Your job is to befriend him. Gain his trust. Whatever you do, don't fall for him. Don't sleep with him. Just friends."

That is the weirdest thing I have ever been asked to do. I frowned. "Why am I doing this?" I asked, feeling confused.

"Because I'm paying you $50,000 to do it, that's why," he replied bluntly, his tone leaving no room for argument.

My heart skipped a beat at the mention of the hefty sum. "$50,000?" I repeated doubtfully, taking a deep breath to steady myself. "To become friends with that guy?" I questioned, pointing to the man.

"Yes," my boss confirmed, his expression unwavering. "I'll give you $15,000 now, and in about a year, you'll relocate to Savannah, Georgia and then convince him to move there. I don't care how you do it. Break his relationship up if he's in one. I don't care what you do, just get him to move to Georgia, and you'll get the other $35,000."

I felt a knot form in my stomach at the magnitude of the task laid out before me. "But... why?" I stammered, struggling to understand.

My boss sighed. "Let's just say Zyler Dixon is special, and it's time for him to come home. I'm getting paid a lot of money to complete this task. I'm willing to pay you to help. But remember," he added, his voice growing stern, "do not fall in love with him. And do not tell him *anything* about this."

"Understood," I replied, my voice tinged with uncertainty.

He stared at me for a moment, then asked, "Well, what are you waiting for?"

"Right now?" I gasped.

"Yes! Right now! If you manage to pull this off and get his number, you'll have $15,000 in your account on Friday."

*Great!* I have never had to get a guy's number. They usually get mine. Is this some kind of reverse prostitution? I'll pay you to be friends with that guy, but don't sleep with him. *Here goes nothing!*

As I stepped out of his sleek black sedan, the crisp autumn air bit at my skin, sending shivers down my spine. Goosebumps prickled along my arms as I glanced back at my boss. His stern nod was all the encouragement I needed to keep moving forward. Taking a deep breath, I squared my shoulders and started toward this Zyler guy. My heart pounded in my chest, each beat louder than the last. Doubts swirled in my mind—*am I making a huge mistake? If this guy ends up dead, I will feel so bad.*

Pushing aside my doubts, I quickened my pace, closing the distance between myself and Zyler. I caught his eye.

"Hey," I flashed a playful smile, infusing a touch of flirtation into my voice as I offered my hand. "I'm Stacy. Since we're both flying solo today, wanna wander around together?"

I don't know how that line worked, but it did.

# CHAPTER 11

STACY

**PRESENT DAY**

Sitting alone in my apartment, I wrestled with my thoughts. Thoughts of Zyler. Thoughts of the strange task my boss had given me. Thoughts of the missing man I had just googled who seemed to be at the center of it all. *Maybe he lost his memory, and he really is the missing man. My boss did say it was time for him to come home.*

Despite my best efforts to keep my feelings at bay, I couldn't deny the truth any longer. I had feelings for Zyler. Deep, undeniable feelings that had been bubbling beneath the surface since the moment I met him.

I didn't know what was going on or why they had me lure him this way. I hadn't received the money yet to get him to move here. I don't give a crap about the money. Not anymore! What matters is that Zyler deserves to know the truth. He deserves to know that I had been sent to befriend him, to manipulate him, to use him for my gain. Despite my boss's warnings to keep feelings out of it, it was too late—I was already in too deep. Part of me loves Zyler. *I have to tell him.* I picked up my phone and sent him a text:

> I LOOKED AND I SEE WHAT YOU ARE TALKING ABOUT. THAT MISSING MAN LOOKS EXACTLY LIKE YOU. I HAVE TO TALK TO YOU IN PERSON. I HAVEN'T BEEN COMPLETELY HONEST WITH YOU, AND I NEED YOU TO KNOW SOMETHING.

He isn't responding. *Ugh! I should call him.* He picked up the phone right away.

"I just saw your text. When do you wanna talk?"

*What if my apartment is bugged?* "Hey Zy, meet me at Lake Mayer Park in two hours. After our chat there, you need to see something in my shed."

"Sounds good. See you soon!"

# Chapter 12

## ZYLER

As I pulled up to Lake Mayer Park, my stomach felt like a tying contest was going on. *Wow! Beautiful place.* The park was serene, bathed in the golden light of late afternoon. I stepped out of the truck and scanned the area, searching for any sign of Stacy.

The only people in sight were a man and a little boy, their laughter rumbling across the park. I smiled at the sight—the unique interaction between a father and son brought back memories of my own dad.

Glancing at my watch, I checked to see if it had been two hours since I talked to Stace. I had arrived early, eager to hear what she had to tell me. Not like I had anything else to do.

The lake shimmered in the distance, its surface rippling gently in the breeze. *I should come here more often.*

I heard the little boy's voice, filled with excitement. "Dad, watch this!" he exclaimed, his small figure darting across the grass.

I quietly chuckled to myself, watching the little dude bust out some crazy Superman move. *I could really use Superman to swoop in and save the day right about now. Hey, buddy, once you're done goofing around, you're welcome to swoop in and save me from the hell I've entered.* If it were only that easy.

I plopped down on the worn bench overlooking the lake. Time was dragging like a snail on a sidewalk. She should have been here fifteen minutes ago. *Where is she? Did she blow me off?*

With each passing second, my anxiety mounted, a gnawing sense of unease settling in my gut. I checked my watch for what felt like the hundredth time, trying to avoid the sinking realization that she wasn't going to show. Dread clawed at the edges of my mind. *Did something happen to her? I hope she didn't crash her car or something. That would be a real bummer!* I tried to kick those pesky negative thoughts out of my brain, but they just kept sneaking back in like an annoying mosquito.

I glanced around, the empty parking lot stretching before me like a deserted wasteland. No sign of her car. Frustration bubbled up inside me as I whipped out my phone and dialed her number. Straight to voicemail. *Fantastic.*

An uneasy feeling settled in the pit of my stomach. Maybe I should go to her house. She mentioned wanting to show me something in the shed. I stood up, determination fueling my steps as I made my way back to the truck.

But as I reached for the door handle, realization struck like a lightning bolt. I don't know where she lives. I cursed under my breath, facepalming in disbelief. Of course, her address is on that damn piece of paper in the house.

I weighed my options, frustration and indecision warring within me. Going back there is the last thing I want to do. But if something happened to Stacy, I can't just sit around twiddling my thumbs. With a heavy sigh, I made up my mind. Looks like I'm heading back to the house.

As I made my way back to my place to grab the address, I decided to give the realtor a call. She did say not to hesitate to reach out to her for any reason. Well, she lied to me. I'd say that is a good reason.

"Hello?" came the realtor's voice over the line.

"Hi, it's Zyler Dixon," I replied, my voice tinged with urgency. "The guy you sold the house to yesterday. I need to talk to you about something. The former house owner... she is very much alive and refusing to leave the house."

There was a brief pause before the realtor let out a surprised laugh. "That's not possible," she said. "Vanessa Marsh passed away. I saw the death certificate."

*Death certificate?* I creased my brows, confusion swirled in my mind. "But... I talked to her," I insisted. "She is there."

The realtor's laughter faded, replaced by a note of concern. "I think you might be mistaken," she said gently. "Maybe you're seeing things."

I rolled my eyes so hard, I thought they were gonna pop out of my head. She's useless. I don't have time to play around. I dropped the call.

As I continued to drive, my thoughts were interrupted by a flicker of movement in the rearview mirror. My heart skipped a beat as I saw a car following closely behind me. *Is this dude following me?*

I turned into my yard, and the car drove by. I let out a shaky breath of relief. "Okay, maybe I'm just being paranoid," I muttered to myself.

*Vanessa is coming with me. I need to see if Stacy can physically see her.*

"Vanessa?" I called out as I entered the house. There was no response, just silence.

*Where did she go?* The question echoed in my mind, a nagging sense of unease creeping over me. *Of course, when I actually need her, she is gone. How convenient.*

A dose of realization struck me. I'd never seen Vanessa's car. If she were actually here, wouldn't there be a vehicle parked outside? The absence of any car only added to my growing confusion.

But there was no time to dwell on it. I swiped the paper off the table and did a quick walk-through of the house, hoping to catch a glimpse of her. But she was nowhere to be seen, as if she'd evaporated into thin air.

With a heavy sigh, I made my way toward my truck.

Attempted to call Stacy once more, but the call was immediately diverted to voicemail. What a stroke of bad luck—have three women giving me a headache today, and I'm not banging any of them. *Geez, maybe I am married.*

# Chapter 13

I pulled up to Stacy's place, my confusion mounting as I realized she lived in an apartment. *What shed was she talking about then?* The pieces of this puzzle were becoming increasingly muddled.

With a sense of urgency devouring me, I made my way to her apartment door and pressed the buzzer. Silence greeted me. I frowned, glancing around anxiously. Her car was parked in the lot, a silent witness to my growing unease. *She has to be here.* I pressed the buzzer again. No response. Struggling to keep my nerves in check, I pressed a few more buzzers, desperate for someone to answer and grant me entry. Finally, one person pushed the buzzer, granting me access to the building. Three people answered through the speaker... Who is it?... Leave me alone, Mike... Yes?

I climbed the stairs to her floor, each step echoing like a drumbeat in the silent hallway. I stood there a moment before I knocked on her door.

*Bang! Bang!* Again, nothing.

With a sinking feeling in my gut, I tried the doorknob and was shocked to find that it was unlocked. Stacy wouldn't mind if I just walked in. She has told me to do it before.

Stepping inside her apartment, my heart plummeted like a stone in my chest. It was like a scene from a night-mare—a tornado had torn through, leaving destruction in its wake. Furniture lay overturned, belongings scattered haphazardly across the floor. But what chilled me to the bone were the stains, dark and ominous, on the carpet. *Blood!*

"Oh my god!" The words escaped my lips in a horrified whisper. This was a crime scene, there was no denying it. Nausea churned in my stomach, threatening to overwhelm me.

Without hesitation, I fumbled for my phone, fingers

shaking as I dialed the emergency number. "I need to report an emergency," I blurted out, the urgency in my voice betraying my fear. "My friend... she didn't show up to meet me, so I came to check on her. Her car's here, but her place... it's destroyed. And there's blood."

There was a brief moment of silence on the other end of the line, then the dispatcher's voice broke through, calm and reassuring. "Sir, I need you to stay calm," she said. "Tell me your friend's address. We'll send help right away."

I relayed the address as quickly as I could, my words tumbling out in a rush. The dispatcher assured me that help was on the way and instructed me to stay put until they arrived. Trembling, I hung up the phone and sank to the floor, my mind reeling with fear and uncertainty.

Tears stung my eyes. "Stacy!" I called out, my voice trembling with fear. The minutes dragged on like hours as I paced the room, my mind consumed with visions of the worst possible scenarios.

Panic surged through me like a tidal wave. *I need to get out of here before the cops arrive.* The last thing I need is to be mistaken for the missing guy and thrust into suspicions I'm not prepared to face. It wouldn't paint a pretty picture if a guy who disappeared for two years suddenly turns up at a bloody crime scene.

Frantically, I scanned the wreckage of her apartment, my heart pounding in my ears. It felt like an elephant was sitting on my chest, crushing the air from my lungs. My eyes fell upon a picture of Stacy and me in a frame on the shelf by the TV. A solitary tear trickled down my cheek as I looked at the photo. She kept that picture—that was a wonderful day.

A day spent lounging at Stacy's house, lazily watching a movie called "Did You Hear About The Morgans?" The film was about an ex-couple forced into witness protection after witnessing a crime, and we had joked and bantered through it, imagining ourselves in their shoes.

Amidst the laughter, I had asked Stacy a question. "If you could start over as a new person, what would you pick as your name?"

Her response had been unexpected, yet oddly fitting. "Seanna," she said with a grin.

I had never heard that name before, but in that moment, it seemed to suit her perfectly—unique, pretty, and full of mystery. In return, I had shared my own choice, "Phoenix." A symbol of rebirth and resilience.

The day Stacy moved had left a void in my life, a pang of longing that I had suppressed out of respect for Jordana. Stacy has been one of the best friends I have ever had. My eyes started to get blurry. *I need to get out of here.*

As I approached the door, I noticed a key rack, and a surge of hope washed over me. There it was... a key marked *shed.*

Without hesitation, I snatched the key from its hook and made a dash out the door. Every second I stayed here increased the likelihood of being caught in the crosshairs of a police investigation. With one last glance over my shoulder, I slipped out of the building. I darted across the parking lot, my heart pounding in my chest as I reached my truck. With trembling hands, I fumbled the key into the ignition and peeled out of the parking lot. *Just in time.*

I could see the cops turning onto her road as I headed in the opposite direction. With my legs shaking, I had to pull over and compose myself.

While sitting in my truck, I couldn't hold back my emotions any longer and started crying. I shouted at the sky, "What has Stacy done wrong? She's a good person.

She doesn't deserve this crap." I lowered my head onto the steering wheel. *She has to be alive. She can't be...*

At that moment, the fear of losing her made me realize that I am in love with her. So much so, I moved across the country just to be close to her.

I sat, paralyzed. Two *burning* questions lingered in my mind. *Where did Vanessa go? And who is after Stacy?* Another thought pierced my mind. *I forgot my damn water bottle in her apartment.*

# CHAPTER 14

I quickly pulled into the driveway, barely avoiding hitting the flowerpot by the step.

"Vanessa?" I called out again, but there was still silence. *I'm losing my damn mind.*

With a quick shower, I tried to shake off the disturbing feeling that lingered from being near the blood. The water cascading over me didn't wash away the unease, but at least I felt cleaner when I stepped out of the bathroom, towel-drying my hair.

I poured myself a drink, contemplating whether I should just drink the whole dang bottle. I couldn't shake Stacy from my mind. Taking a sip of my drink, I sat on the couch. Stacy's face haunted me, and tears welled up in my eyes once more. *I can't lose her.*

*What was she going to tell me? Was she going to confess feelings for me?* God, I hope so. In my mind, I begged for her to be *alive.*

I heard a faint noise coming from above, like a soft shuffling sound. Curiosity piqued; I followed the sound until I reached a door leading to the attic. With a sense of apprehension, I grabbed a nearby chair and positioned it under the attic door.

As I climbed up and pushed the door open, a rush of cool air greeted me, and I peered into the darkness of the attic. My heart pounded in my chest as I tried to detect the source of the noise, expecting to find some small creature scurrying about.

Out of nowhere, a whisper pierced the stillness, beckoning me by name.

"Zyler?"

I froze, my hand still gripping the attic door.

"Is that you?"

I jumped at the unexpected sound. My head collided with the edge of the attic opening. "Ouch! What the hell, Vanessa?" I exclaimed, my voice filled with surprise and pain. "What are you doing up here?"

She inched closer and extended her hand. "I'll show you," she said, with a mysterious glint in her eyes.

I motioned for her to drop her hand and moved up beside her. "Show me what?" I asked.

She pointed to the corner of the room. There, on the wall, a big screen for watching projector films stood, surrounded by a stack of good old videos. A cozy blanket draped over a couple of squishy chairs that looked like they could give great hugs completed the setup.

"What is that?" I asked, my eyes widening with curiosity.

"That's one of our special spots in the house," Vanessa shared, her voice quivering with emotion as she fought back tears. "We'd come up here and watch our videos together. Our wedding video, camping videos, the last video of my mom..."

I couldn't tell if it was the alcohol from the drink I downed coursing through my veins, the overwhelming dread of losing my friend, or perhaps my own sanity slipping away, but witnessing the anguish in Vanessa's eyes truly crushed my soul. In my desperation to defend myself against the mistaken identity of her husband, I had completely overlooked her feelings in all of this.

Stacy had been missing for a few hours, and I felt like an utter mess. It had been two distressing years since this poor girl last had last seen her husband. Gently, I reached out, taking her hand in mine. She glanced at our joined hands, then met my eyes.

"Vanessa, I apologize..." I sighed heavily, the weight of the situation pressing down on me. "For everything today. The way I handled this whole situation. I should have done it differently."

*Oh, no! Why are you looking at me weird?*

She squeezed my hand and took a deep breath, her expression landing with a frown. "You really don't re-member any of it, do you?" she said with a look in her eyes, as if pleading for a miracle.

I looked at her, the weight of her sadness palpable in the air. "I don't. I'm sorry!" I wanted so badly to say, *because it wasn't me*, but I knew it would only rub salt in her wounds. So instead, I played along. "Can you show me the videos of us? Not the wedding one, the other ones. The moments that made us, well... us." I held my breath, hoping she wouldn't start crying again.

*Phew, thank heavens!* She smiled for once. "I thought

you'd never ask." With newfound energy, she sprang into action, setting up the videos. Then she gestured to a chair and quipped, "This bad boy is yours."

I plopped down on the seat. It felt like sinking into a cloud. *I definitely would remember this old thing.*

As I watched them fooling around at the campsite, my heart clenched as he ran up and swooped her into his arms, kissing her on the forehead while swinging her around. They looked so happy together. Tears formed in my eyes as I realized I was witnessing a relationship that I had only ever dreamt of. It was like watching myself living out the dream of being unbelievably happy, yet I couldn't recall ever feeling the joy that was written all over the face that looked exactly like mine.

I glanced at Vanessa. Her eyes glistened with tears. *Say something!* I told myself. What do you say in a moment like this? "He really..." I noticed she gave me a glare. I cleared my throat. *Just say it!* "We really loved each other, didn't we?"

She stared at the screen, her gaze fixed on the memories playing out before us. "More than anyone could love another person," she whispered.

"I don't understand. If you were that happy, why

would he…" I shook my head. "I mean, why would I leave?"

She looked at me, her eyes searching mine for answers. "I have asked myself that over a thousand times, Zyler. There was only one logical reason, and that was that you—"

"Didn't leave willingly?" I finished her sentence.

She nodded, her expression grave. "I'd bet my life on that."

This is sad as hell. It is so heartbreaking I can't even argue that it wasn't me at this point.

*Son of a fucking gun! My water bottle.* The cops are going to think I am a suspect. I need to get the hell out of here.

I turned to face Vanessa. "I have to make a trip back to Nevada tomorrow. There are a few things I need to wrap up there."

She squinted at me, suspicion flickering in her eyes. "Seriously? You are leaving me… again."

"It's important," I insisted, feeling the weight of guilt hit me like a sucker punch. I can't just ditch her in this emotional state. I still need to prove to her that I am not who she thinks I am.

I reached out and grabbed her arm, pleading, "Will you come with me?"

# CHAPTER 15

## VANESSA

### TWO YEARS AGO

"That was fun, babe!" I grinned as we exited the bowling alley.

"I'm glad you enjoyed it, beautiful. Now, onto the next adventure," Zyler announced with a mischievous twinkle in his eyes.

With the golden rays of the sun starting to illuminate Savannah, Georgia, Zyler and I ventured towards the zip lining park nestled deep within the trees. The smell of pine trees filled the air, and the fresh coffee aroma wafted from a little café nearby.

As we got closer to the entrance, the lively conversation and laughter of other thrill-seekers getting ready for their own zip lining adventures filled me with an electric rush of anticipation.

Zyler pointed to the magnificent trees, whose branches were fluttered with the wind as we prepared to race through them. We could hear the distant sound of a swift-moving creek. A rush of exhilaration shot through me as we got closer to the starting point. Zip lining had a slightly terrifying element mixed with excitement.

When I stepped off of the platform, the world below me turned into a flurry of movement as I shot through the sky. As I soared above the treetops, my blood pounded with adrenaline, the thrilling wind in my ears drowned out all other sounds. I'd never experienced anything like the thrill of zip lining before. It was intense.

As I got to the finish line, my face broke into a huge smile. My veins were prickling with excitement and triumph. "Wow, that was absolutely incredible!" I exclaimed. "I can't believe we did that! What a rush!"

Zyler squeezed my hand. "I love creating these memories with you."

"Thanks for the most amazing day. I love you."

"It really was a good day, wasn't it? I love you, too," he replied.

As we drove back home, the conversation turned serious. "Do you think we're ready for kids?" I asked hesitantly.

Zyler glanced at me out of the corner of his eye. "I think we are. We will rock as parents."

Once inside the house, I headed straight for the bathroom. "I'm going to take a bath, babe," I called out.

"I'll quickly run into town and grab us some Chinese food. Probably be back before you even get out," Zyler replied, planting a kiss on my forehead.

"Don't forget the extra shrimp on mine!" I teased, hugging him tightly.

"Never," Zyler promised. I didn't realize he told me he loved me until he was already gone.

The bath felt heavenly on my sore muscles. I must have pulled something zip lining. I couldn't stop imagining how amazing Zyler would be as a father. After the bath, I slipped into my new satin red nightgown. He is going to love this.

While pouring two drinks, I glanced at the clock. "He

should be back by now," I muttered to myself. It must be busy tonight at the restaurant.

The anticipation was noticeable as I walked through the living room. The soft glow of the candlelight cast flickering shadows on the walls, creating a romantic ambiance. I couldn't help but smile, thinking about our day—how Zyler's laughter mingled with the sounds of the forest, the rush of wind as we soared through the treetops, and the exhilaration of experiencing something new together.

I sat on the couch, setting the drinks on the coffee table. The scent of pine and earth still lingered in my senses, intertwined with the sweet, warm aroma of vanilla candles I lit.

He should be here any minute, I thought, glancing at the clock again. My heart fluttered with anticipation. I envisioned the look on his face when he saw me in the nightgown.

Another thirty minutes ticked by. Where the hell is he? I called his cell. I heard it buzz on the table. He forgot it. I sighed, trying to quell the rising unease in my chest.

Two more hours passed by. Panic flooded my mind. Something is wrong. I dialed the police.

"Hello, this is Vanessa Dixon. I think something happened to my husband," I blurted out, trying to hold it together. My voice wavered with panic, and the call was a mess, but the dispatcher assured me that the cops were going to swing by.

As I waited for the police to arrive, I paced back and forth, my mind racing with worst-case scenarios. I couldn't bear the thought of not knowing where Zyler was. Each minute felt like an eternity, my heart pounding in my chest like a relentless drum.

The house, which had felt so comforting and warm just moments ago, now seemed eerily quiet and foreboding. Shadows stretched across the walls, and every creak and groan of the old wood amplified my anxiety. I kept glancing at the door, willing it to open and reveal Zyler's reassuring presence, but it remained stubbornly shut.

I tried to focus, to piece together anything that might explain his disappearance. *Had someone taken him? Was he hurt?* The unanswered questions grated on me, each one more terrifying than the last.

I collapsed onto the couch, tears streaming down my face. The sound of the doorbell interrupted my despair. I rushed to the door, throwing it open just as the police officers stepped out of their car.

"Mrs. Dixon?" one of them asked, his expression a mix of professionalism and concern.

"Yes, please, come in," I responded. "I can't find my husband. He was supposed to be back by now, and I... I just know something's wrong."

The officers entered, their presence bringing a slight but temporary sense of relief. They began asking questions, trying to piece together the timeline of events.

"Did he say where he was going?" one officer inquired.

"He confirmed he was going to get Chinese food and that he would be right back," I replied, my voice trembling. "But he should have been back hours ago. That..." My voice cracked. "That usually only takes him around twenty minutes."

As they took notes, I felt a sudden chill run down my spine. The fear of the unknown was suffocating, and I couldn't shake the feeling that time was slipping away. Every second counted, and with each passing moment, the dread deepened.

"We'll start by checking the restaurant and his usual route," the lead officer confirmed, his tone firm and reassuring. "We'll do everything we can to find him."

I nodded, trying to muster some semblance of hope. "Thank you," I managed to say, my eyes welling up with tears.

As the officers left to begin their search, I sank onto the couch, clutching Zyler's favorite jacket. As the minutes ticked by, I prayed that he would walk through the door, safe and sound.

Nights turned into days, and the search for Zyler dragged on with no new leads. The world outside moved forward, but my life felt frozen in place, stuck in the agonizing uncertainty of his absence.

I tossed and turned in bed, haunted by memories of our last moments together. We were going to try for a family. When he told me he loved me, I never said it back. The regret chipped at my heart, an endless loop of "what ifs" played in my mind.

Desperation consumed me, my every thought fixated on finding him. I wandered through our empty home, my fingers trailing over photographs of happier times. Tears stained the memories, blurring the faces of our smiles.

In the kitchen, I lingered over the table where we had shared countless meals and dreams for the future. In the living room, I sat on the couch where we had laughed and held each other through countless nights. Everywhere I looked, the ghosts of our past seemed to whisper his name, intensifying the ache in my heart.

The house felt like a tomb, silent and oppressive. I found myself talking to him as if he could hear me, my voice echoing through the rooms. "Zyler, where are you? Please come back to me."

The nights were the hardest, filled with sleepless hours. I clung to the hope that he would walk through the door, and I would see his smile and hear his voice again. The thought of *never* seeing him again was unbearable.

"I promise," I whispered between sobs, "if you ever come back, I will never leave your side again."

# CHAPTER 16

## ZYLER

"So, what do you say? Will you come with me?" I asked.

She appeared both confused and shocked. "Of course, I'm coming with you."

I sighed in relief. "Good!"

"I'm just glad you are taking me with you this time."

*Wow! She really went there.* "Okay! No need to go there."

"You're right," she said, her tone softening. "Thank you for asking me to come." She stepped forward and wrapped her arms around me in a tight hug.

"Oh, umm... no problem," I replied, awkwardly patting her on the back like she was a long-lost buddy of mine.

Vanessa pulled back slightly, her voice breaking the silence. "So, when are we leaving?"

"We're leaving first thing in the morning," I said. The sooner we get out of here, the sooner we could start unraveling this mess. And maybe, just maybe, find some answers.

I sighed inwardly. Sleeping in a house with a woman I barely know, who is convinced we are married and had been intimate in nearly every room—well, it was certainly a new experience for me. I decided to sleep on the couch instead of using either of the beds.

We loaded up the truck at 6:00 a.m. and hit the road. It didn't take long for our differing music tastes to surface. Vanessa questioned why I had switched off the country station she had tuned in to.

"Because country music isn't really my thing," I admitted.

She looked at me with disbelief, a small frown forming on her lips. "So, you were just pretending to like my music?" she asked skeptically.

I shot her a glance, feeling a surge of irritation. "For heaven's sake, no," I retorted. "I would never pretend to like something for someone else. I guess I went through a country phase for a while and just never got back into it," I said, defeated, clicking the country station back on. *Great. Hours of listening to this depressing crap. I should have left her at the house.*

My first plan was to see if anyone else could see her or if I had gone completely schizophrenic. Perfect timing—the truck needs gas. I pulled over to a gas station and had her come inside the store with me to grab some snacks.

As we strolled down the aisle, I suggested to Vanessa, "Hey, why don't you grab something to drink?"

A passing lady gave me a strange look, making me question my own sanity. The way she looked at me, you'd think I was talking to myself. *Maybe I am seeing things.*

I turned to the woman and gestured towards Vanessa. "Ma'am, can you see her?" I asked, desperation creeping into my voice.

Vanessa let out an exasperated huff and shot me a glare.

"Of course she can see me."

The woman's confusion only deepened, and I pressed on, needing reassurance. "I need to know," I insisted, my heart pounding. "Can you see her too? Is she actually alive?"

A flicker of fear crossed the woman's face as she glanced between Vanessa and me. "Are you okay?" she asked Vanessa.

Vanessa chuckled, a hint of sarcasm in her tone. "Oh, I'm fine," she reassured the woman. "Don't mind him. This is my husband. He disappeared for two years, heard I was dead, then decided to come back home. Now he's curious if I'm actually still alive or if he's seeing things."

The woman's eyes widened in disbelief before she hastily pulled out her cell phone. I exchanged a knowing look with Vanessa, realizing the lady was probably calling the cops.

"Really, Vanessa?" I muttered under my breath. "We've got to go."

With that, we swiftly made our exit. "You're the one asking all the crazy questions," she said as she climbed into the truck.

"Well, you made it seem like I skipped town and hired

a hitman to take you out."

She gasped. "I never even thought of that," she paused and eyed me, "did you?"

"What the hell... of course not."

She laughed. "I'm just messing with you, relax."

I considered turning myself in for anything I could be charged with. Jail sounds more appealing than a road trip with her.

# CHAPTER 17

As I checked the time, I groaned, knowing I still had two hours of torture ahead of me on this never-ending drive. Man, I never thought I'd be praying for an end to a road trip so badly! As the minutes ticked by, I could feel my patience slowly slipping away. I caught myself daydreaming about making a pit stop at the Grand Canyon and debating whether to drive myself off the edge, or perhaps tossing her off instead. Both options were looking rather good by now.

I couldn't help but think that her constant yapping could be the reason her husband hit the road. *I'm going to hell for thinking that.*

"Zyler, when you said that I'm not your type, what did you mean by that?"

I let out a massive sigh. "Fuck me!" I muttered through my teeth.

"I would, but according to you, I'm not your type."

My head spun so fast I think it gave me whiplash. I looked at her with a *'for the love of God, please shut up'* look. She's smiling. *She thinks this is funny.*

I cleared my throat. "What I meant is I'm done with brunettes for a while. Bad experiences. Moving onto blondes." Stacy fit the bill perfectly. She's the only girl on my radar.

"So, you are saying my hair color is a deal breaker?"

It's better if she thinks that. I don't want to hurt her feelings by admitting that I prefer women with a little extra cushion—a nice, plump booty. I'm not shallow, though. A killer personality makes a woman a total knockout in my eyes. I've dated women of all shapes and sizes; I'm an equal opportunity ex-collector. Women are attractive in their own ways, but like everyone else, I have my preferences.

"No, Vanessa. I just don't feel like our personalities click. Your looks aren't the deal breaker here. You are very pretty. Just not..."

"Your type. I get it, Zyler. I don't know why you bothered marrying me in the first place."

I sighed deeply, feeling defeated. I was going to wait for this, but I need to do it now. It's a tough decision, especially since I've been in a long-term standoff with my mom. We had a tiff, and neither of us wanted to be the first to apologize.

Here goes nothing. I called my mom through the Bluetooth speaker. I needed someone other than me to break the news to this girl that I'm not her husband.

"Zyler?"

"Yes, Mom, it's me."

"I'm so happy to hear from you."

"Same, Mom."

"Hi, Mrs. Dixon," Vanessa hollered.

"Who is that?"

"It's my friend, Vanessa."

Vanessa coughed. "It's his wife."

I shot her a serious look, hoping she would stop talking.

"Wife?" my mom said, giggling.

"Mom, can you please tell this woman that she is not

my wife? That I have never been married."

My mom was giving me the silent treatment on the phone. She was probably fuming, thinking I eloped without telling her.

"Oh, I see. This is some type of role-play thing."

"What? No, Mom."

She whispered into the speaker, "Zyler, friend-zoning is no way to treat your wife."

"Not my wife, Mom!"

"Vanessa, he's your friend, remember? Or did you forget to update your friendship settings?" My mom joked. I swear I could feel her wink coming through the phone and poking me in the eye.

"Hey Mom, gotta run, but just wanted to let you know your favorite disappointment is still alive and kickin'!"

*Well, that was useless.* I shook my head in frustration and glanced up, seeing a sign that said, "65 miles." *Thank the universe! Just one more hour.* I stepped on the gas, willing to risk a ticket.

"Your mom sounds like a riot. I think we would get along great. I always hoped you would let me meet her," Vanessa said.

I gave up. Not even responding at this point.

As we cruised into the city, I hightailed it to Jordana's workplace. If anyone could confirm that I've been causing havoc in her life for the past three years, it was definitely her. This would totally prove to Vanessa that there's no way I could have bailed on her two years back.

Walking in, Jordana wasted no time giving me attitude and throwing shade. "Watch this one, he's a runner," she quipped.

"That's not true, Jordana... you were the one," I started to deny, but caught myself. "It doesn't matter."

She turned to Vanessa and delivered another punchline. "Don't be shocked if he can't remember a single important date or if he disappears and you don't hear from him until he randomly pops back up one day. Like right now."

I let out a huge sigh, trying to act all chill. "Oh, come on! You're the one who ditched me for that Chad dude after cheating on me."

"Yeah, I heard you were gonna flake on me and move to Georgia. So, I thought I'd beat you to it and start moving on first," Jordana fired back.

"What? Who told you that nonsense?" I demanded, crossing my arms.

"Who do you think? Your friend that you wouldn't stop yammering on about, claiming she was just a buddy when it was obvious you were head over heels for her."

"I didn't decide to move to Georgia until after you left me," I insisted.

She chuckled, like a cat hacking up a hairball. "Keep lying. I'm over it."

"I don't understand why Stacy would tell you I was moving before I even talked to her about it," I said, feeling confused and frustrated.

Jordana threw her hands up in the air. "Probably obsessed with you and wanted you for herself. I don't know. Ask her."

She looked at Vanessa. "Good luck trying to take Stacy's place. He was totally smitten with her. I guess he just stuck around with me so he wouldn't look like a total jerk ditching his girl for someone else," she snapped, giving me the death stare.

"Wow! I'm sorry you saw it that way. I loved you, Jordana. I would have never moved if you didn't... I had intentions of marrying you one day."

"Keep telling yourself that if it makes you feel better. Just so you know, Zyler, you mumble some interesting things in your sleep. Let's just say, it definitely wasn't me starring in your dreams."

"Funny, I don't recall ever having dreams."

"Face the truth. I bring up kids once and suddenly you're packing your bags for Georgia with Stacy? You bolted, admit it."

I couldn't breathe. I needed some fresh air. Grabbing Vanessa's hand, I said, "Let's get out of here!"

As we were walking away, Jordana shouted, "You haven't changed. Walk away when things get tough. That's what you are good at."

I flipped her off. As ticked off as I was at Jordana for making me look bad, I was even more baffled by something else. *Why did Stacy tell her that I was going to break it off and move to Georgia?*

# Chapter 18

**Three Days Later**

As I sat in the cramped hotel room in Nevada, frustration plagued me like a relentless beast. It had been a couple of days since we arrived, and my search for answers had led me nowhere. The only breakthrough I had was discovering that the shed was located somewhere in Nevada. Engraved on the back of the key was the unmistakable word: *Nevada.* But the search for it had been futile.

Stacy still hadn't answered her phone. I need to get back to her apartment and see if she had anything else that would shed light on why she acted the way she did and what she was going to tell me that day.

Vanessa is probably itching to go home as well. Honestly, I'd love to drop her off somewhere. After the last seven days with her, I need a break. Despite our differences, we found one thing in common—we both have impeccable taste in movies. This girl is all about action and thrillers, just like me.

With a sense of urgency, I grabbed my phone and quickly Googled the news for any updates from Georgia. What I found shook me to the core. Breaking news flashed across the screen: "Stacy Banks has been missing for six days. DNA in her apartment has come back as the missing man in Pooler, Georgia—Zyler Ray Dixon. If anyone sees this man, contact the police ASAP. He is a person of interest that may have information regarding this case. He is not a suspect at this time. There is also an active missing persons case on him for the last two years."

My heart pounded in my chest as I read and reread the words, my mind reeling with disbelief. *How is this possible?* My DNA matches... I looked at Vanessa... *her husband's. He even has my middle name.*

All I could do was stare at the floor. *I can't go back*

*there now.* I felt paralyzed. I don't understand. *I know I'm not him. I can't be him.* I'm not missing any memories. I remember my entire life—well, since I was like five years old. I wondered if Vanessa had seen the news. She would never believe me then. Not that the people in my life are helping this situation. *I wish Dad were here. He would know what to do.*

I motioned for Vanessa to come sit beside me, my expression grave and earnest. As she settled near me, I took a deep breath, steeling myself for the difficult conversation ahead.

"Vanessa, we need to talk," I began, my voice trembling slightly. "I need you to listen to me, and I need you to believe me."

She gave me a look like she was trying to figure me out and was also low-key worried.

"I know without a doubt I'm not your husband," I confessed. I paused, gathering my thoughts before continuing, "The police found DNA at my friend Stacy's apartment. They say it belongs to your husband. But... it's mine. My picture is there, too."

Tears welled up in my eyes as I pleaded with her, "Please, Vanessa, you have to believe me. I don't understand why our DNA is being linked together. There has to be some kind of mistake, or maybe even a conspiracy."

Reaching out, I desperately took her hands in mine. "I swear to you, I'm not him. He's still out there somewhere. My friend Stacy is missing and possibly hurt really bad. Maybe even..." I couldn't finish the thought. "And I think... I think we might be in danger."

Vanessa's eyes glistened with tears as she listened. "This is so hard to believe," she admitted, her voice trembling with emotion, "but I'll try. What do we do now?"

I reached into my pocket and pulled out the key, holding it up for her to see. "The last thing Stacy said to me was she wanted to show me something in her shed," I explained. "I don't know what shed she was referring to, but this was at her place, so I swiped it. I have a feeling the shed is somewhere in this city." I let out a weary sigh, squeezing my chin with my hand. "I just don't know where."

Vanessa's eyes widened as she examined the key. "It looks like a storage shed key," she declared.

Her words caused a light bulb to go off in my head. "Storage shed!" I exclaimed, relief flooding through me. "I didn't even think of that. I was imagining the type of shed in a backyard to store a lawnmower in."

Without hesitation, I pulled her into my arms. "Vanessa, you're a genius," I declared, squeezing her tightly before pulling back. Shaking the key in front of us, I proclaimed, "We need to find this."

# Chapter 19

## STACY

### Six Months Ago

The more I get to know Zyler, the more I want to back out of this arrangement. He seems genuinely happy with his girlfriend, and they're getting quite serious. *I refuse to be the cause of their breakup.*

I met up with my boss to negotiate the terms.

"I can't go through with this. I don't want the money," I whimpered, my hands shaking uncontrollably in my lap.

"If you don't convince him to move to Georgia like

planned, there will no longer be an active bank account to put money in. Catch my drift."

I couldn't breathe. My heart felt like it had jumped out of my throat. "I understand. I'll continue as planned."

I went home and cried myself to sleep.

A week later, I met up with Zyler's girlfriend, Jordana. I knew the only way he would move was if they broke up, so I did what I had to do. My life depended on it. I told Jordana that Zyler planned to leave her and move to Georgia with me. After walking away from her that day, I cried in my car. *He's going to hate me, and I wouldn't blame him.*

Curiosity gnawed at me, driving me to uncover the truth behind my boss's interest in Zyler. With my boss out of state on a trip, I seized the opportunity to investigate further, knowing I had a small window of opportunity without his prying eyes. Manipulating the security cameras to conceal my presence, I delved into the depths of his office undetected.

Growing up with a father in security had its advantages, and I made sure to exploit them to the fullest. As I rummaged through the papers in a cabinet adjacent to my boss's desk, my eyes fell on a file labeled *"Lynette Bolton,"* and my curiosity peaked. Flipping it open, I was not prepared for what I was about to see. Photos of Zyler, taken everywhere—snapshots that seemed to follow his every move. *What the hell is this? Why is he being followed?*

Quickly, I snapped photos of the documents with my camera, ensuring I had evidence of what I had found. A hat caught my eye on a nearby shelf, stirring a sense of familiarity as I realized it was the same one from one of the photos. It must belong to Zyler. *Who is he? Better yet... who the hell is my boss? Psycho stalker, that's who he is.*

With my heart racing, I hurriedly restored everything to its original state, ensuring there was no trace of my intrusion. Well, almost. I know it was unbelievably stupid, but I had to take the hat. Scurrying out of his office, I locked everything up and made sure the security camera would reset to normal in five minutes. Stripping off the rubber gloves, I shoved them into my jeans pocket.

I glanced over my shoulder, half-expecting to see someone lurking in the darkness, watching my every move.

Paranoia crept over me like a suffocating blanket. Reaching my car, I fumbled with the keys, my hands trembling with adrenaline-fueled fear. Every sound freaked me out.

I ripped out of the parking lot, the tires screeching against the asphalt as I raced away. The city lights blurred past in a dizzying haze. Dread settled deep in the pit of my stomach. I should have never gotten involved in this. Why did I agree to something so crazy? There is no turning back now.

The next day, I made my way to the nearest storage facility. I had been considering renting a unit for the move, realizing that I wouldn't be able to take everything right away. Now seemed like the perfect time.

At the storage facility, I rented a small unit. The attendant handed me the key, and I wasted no time in stashing a box with the camera, the hat, and all the incriminating evidence inside. Until I could figure out what to do with it all, the storage shed would serve as a temporary hiding place.

With that taken care of, my focus shifted to Lynette Bolton. I was desperate to uncover the identity of this woman, unravel her ties to Zyler, and untangle her mysterious link to my boss.

Locating Lynette proved to be a challenge. It took hours of digging and searching, but eventually, I managed to find her address and place of work. The timing couldn't have been worse, as I was scheduled to move to Georgia the following day. I hastily wrote down the information and placed it in the box with the other items. I vowed to come back as soon as possible.

# CHAPTER 20

## ZYLER

Armed with the key, we ventured into the first storage shed area.

"I hope this shed isn't too difficult to find," Vanessa remarked.

"I have a feeling it's going to be worth the search," I replied, flashing her a reassuring smile. But deep down, a knot of apprehension twisted in my gut. What secrets awaited us in that hidden shed?

As we walked toward the storage sheds, Vanessa seemed lost in thought.

"You seem quiet," I observed, breaking the silence that

had settled between us.

Vanessa sighed, a fleeting expression of sadness crossing her features like a passing shadow. "I've just been thinking about my past, about the things I've been through."

I nodded understandingly. "If you ever feel like talking about it, I'm here to listen."

She offered me a grateful smile, a flicker of vulnerability in her eyes. "Thanks. It's just... it's hard to open up considering the circumstances."

"I get that," I replied softly, reaching out to gently squeeze her hand. "I haven't been the easiest to be open with about things. I'll do better going forward."

As we continued our search, Vanessa began to open up, her words tumbling forth like a dam breaking free. She spoke of her childhood, of the struggles she had faced growing up, and of the death of her mother.

I felt a connection form with Vanessa, a shared bond forged through our common experiences of losing a parent. Her mother's death had been slow, a painful ordeal that she was forced to witness. In contrast, my father's passing had been sudden, snatching him away in an instant. That's the difference between cancer and a massive heart attack.

I always felt that my father had been robbed—snatched away at a young age, denied the chance to enjoy his retirement or enjoy grandparenthood. Yet, as Vanessa recounted her mother's agonizing decline, I found myself reconsidering. Perhaps my father's abrupt passing had spared him prolonged suffering. A small blessing in disguise.

As Vanessa stood watch, her eyes scanning the surroundings for any signs of lurking observers, I discreetly tried the keys on the shed locks. Just as I was about to test another lock, the sound of approaching footsteps echoed around the corner.

Quickly regaining my composure, I turned to Vanessa, our eyes meeting in silent understanding. Without missing a beat, we shifted our attention to the approaching figure, putting on our best facade of casual interest. I quickly grabbed Vanessa's hand to give the impression that we were a couple.

"Excuse me, are you two looking to rent a shed?" the person asked, their voice friendly but laced with a hint of suspicion.

Caught off guard, I exchanged a brief glance with

Vanessa before nodding hesitantly. "Uh, yeah, we were just... considering our options," I replied, mentally cursing my lack of improvisation skills.

The person nodded, seemingly satisfied with our response, and proceeded to give us a brief tour of the available sheds.

After they had left us to start the paperwork for our rental, I turned to Vanessa with a grin. "Don't say I never gave you anything," I teased.

Vanessa laughed, a lightness returning to her expression. "Noted."

"You know, this is the first day I've truly enjoyed in a long time," I confessed, feeling a weight lifting off my shoulders.

She nudged my arm gently. "I'd have to agree with that."

The guy ushered us into the office to pay the fee. With a friendly smile, he handed us the key, and we made our way back to the truck. But as I examined the key in my hand, a frown creased my brow. It looked distinctly different from Stacy's key.

"Well, this isn't where it is, because these keys are different," I murmured, disappointment creeping into my voice as I turned to Vanessa.

Her eyes widened with realization. "Wait a minute," she exclaimed, a spark of excitement in her voice. "Why don't we just go to the offices and see if it's one of their keys?"

I blinked in surprise, impressed by her quick thinking. "But how are we going to do that?" I asked, a note of skepticism creeping into my tone. "We can't just say we found it, or they'll take it back."

Vanessa gave me a playful smirk. "Such an amateur," she teased, shaking her head in mock disappointment. "Good thing you have a woman with you."

Her confidence sparked a newfound sense of determination within me as we headed to the next storage facility. Vanessa led the way with assurance, her steps purposeful and resolute. Stepping into the office, she approached the worker with a charming smile.

"Hi there," she began, her tone sweet and innocent. "My sister wanted me to grab something from her shed, but I do not remember if it was this place or the one on Royal Street. Is this a key for here?"

The worker frowned in confusion, examining the key before shaking his head. "No, sorry, it isn't one of ours," he replied. "But that is a key for the storage place on 9th Avenue."

A thrill of excitement surged through me as Vanessa shot me a triumphant grin, and said, "Looks like we're headed to 9th Avenue."

# CHAPTER 21

Vanessa and I scanned the numbers painted on each door, searching for any sign that might lead us to the one we needed.

"Knowing Stacy, she would have picked a number that meant something to her," I remarked, trying to decipher the mystery.

She gave me an incredulous look. "Right! I'll just call her up and ask," Vanessa replied sarcastically.

Chuckling at her response, I considered the possibilities. "Well, there are three numbers I can think of," I said thoughtfully. "Six, for her birthday. Eleven, for the day her grandma passed away. And her favorite number was three."

Vanessa stared at me in disbelief. "Wow," she exclaimed, shaking her head slightly. "It's funny how your memory remembers everything about this girl, down to the numbers in her life."

I chuckled softly. "I can't help what I remember," I protested, though her words struck a chord. There was a hint of jealousy in her tone, and I couldn't help but wonder why.

Raising an eyebrow, Vanessa regarded me skeptically. "Either that, or you're really good at pretending you forget things."

I nudged her playfully with my shoulder, unable to suppress a laugh. "Ah, come on now. No need for that kind of energy around here," I retorted with a grin. "We need to focus. We are so close."

"Thanks to me," she joked, a mischievous twinkle in her eyes.

"Oh, whatever," I muttered, feeling a twinge of irritation as we tried each of the numbers—6, 11, and 3—without success. A sinking feeling settled in the pit of my stomach. "I don't know what other numbers to try," I said, frustration creeping into my voice.

Vanessa placed a reassuring hand on my shoulder. "Just start trying from the beginning."

The more I tried, the more hope I was losing. "It isn't 1-14," I mumbled, feeling increasingly frustrated with each failed attempt.

Before she could respond, a person rounded the corner, unlocking door number 16 and disappearing inside. Vanessa and I exchanged a look of disappointment. "Well, it's not 16," she remarked with a sigh.

I felt a pang of anxiety as I whispered to Vanessa, "We're going to get kicked out before we even find it."

Determined to persevere, Vanessa snatched the key from my hand and approached door number 19. She inserted the key into the lock and turned it. To our surprise, the lock clicked open.

Vanessa turned to me, an enormous smile lighting up her face. "Your birthday," she exclaimed.

I sat there, stunned into silence, my mouth hanging open in disbelief. Vanessa shrugged her shoulders like she does this on a daily basis. "I figured, since it wasn't one of her significant days, and you two have this connection that made her convince you to move, your bond is mutual. Therefore, your birthday was a good guess."

I gotta hand it to Vanessa. She's like a frickin' detective with that intuition of hers. The way she makes connections that the rest of us failed to see. But as I wallowed in the thrill of our success, a wave of sadness draped over me like a soggy blanket. Walking into that shed, filled with Stacy's stuff, I realized I may never get the chance to tell Stacy how I really feel about her.

As we entered the shed, I reached for the light switch and flicked it on, only to be greeted by a musty smell reminiscent of grandpa's old attic. "Yuck," I grimaced, wrinkling my nose in disgust.

I couldn't help but feel a pang of nostalgia as my eyes landed on the worn-out couch nestled in the corner of the shed. "I remember sitting on that so many times," I murmured to Vanessa, my voice tinged with bittersweet reminiscence. "We would hang out and watch movies. Completely platonic, of course," I added quickly, feeling the need to clarify. "I had a girlfriend, and I would never cheat. Not my character."

My attention then shifted to a picture that used to hang on the wall above the couch. "I wonder why she didn't bring that," I said, scratching my head in confusion. Stacy loves that picture.

Before I could dwell on it further, I noticed Vanessa already crouched beside a box in the middle of the floor, her expression tense. With a sense of foreboding, I approached her.

Vanessa looked up at me, her eyes wide with fear. "Um, Zyler, you need to come look at this," she said, her voice trembling slightly.

Curiosity and apprehension mingled within me as I peered into the box. "What is this stuff?"

Vanessa hesitated for a moment before reaching inside the box and pulling out a hat. "It's your stuff."

I noticed her tearing up. "What's wrong? Do you recognize that hat?"

"Don't you?"

"No... should I?" I asked, feeling a knot forming in my stomach.

"It's your... I mean my husband's hat," she explained, her words hanging heavily in the air.

"Oh!" I cried out as I pulled out a camera with a post-it note that read: Zyler's pics.

"My pics? I need to check this out," I muttered, fumbling to turn on the camera. To my surprise, it wasn't dead. I had no idea of the chilling sight that awaited me.

Dozens of pictures of me, in all different places. Some were even with Stacy. I took a sharp breath. She wasn't the one taking them.

"Why does she have so many pictures of me? That's kind of..." I trailed off, unable to find the right word to describe the unsettling feeling that washed over me.

"Creepy!" Vanessa interrupted, finishing my thought with a shudder.

"Yeah," I agreed, my mind racing with questions and possibilities. I noticed a picture of a file with the name Lynette Bolton. "Wonder who that is? Did your husband know a Lynette?"

"Don't think so. He never mentioned the name. Your guess is as good as mine," she replied.

"Looks like Stacy wrote her address and place of work on this post-it."

Vanessa gave me a worried and slightly scared look. "Seems like it. Guess our next step is to find out who this Lynette Bolton is."

# CHAPTER 22

I sat on the edge of the hotel bed, scrolling through the pictures on Stacy's camera. My mind drifted as I relived each moment captured in time. But as I reached a particular photo, a sense of déjà vu washed over me. In the picture, I was walking into a place that looked hauntingly familiar, wearing that hat. But the name of the business was cut off.

"Vanessa, come here a second," I called out. Setting her book aside, she joined me on the bed. "Look at this picture I found. This place looks so familiar, and... I'm wearing that hat."

Checking out the photo in the camera, Vanessa's eyes

widened as she studied the image. There was a moment of silence.

"Is something wrong?" I asked.

Tears streamed down her face as she struggled to catch her breath.

"That's the night you... I mean, he vanished. He went to get Chinese food for us. Never came back," she managed to choke out between sobs, her trembling finger pointing at the picture on the screen. "That's the restaurant."

I put in a solemn effort to recall that moment! I may not be her hubby, but these pics beg to differ! It is me in them. Which means the hat must be mine.

I placed a comforting hand on Vanessa's shoulder, offering her what little solace I could in the face of such overwhelming grief. "I'm so sorry you had to go through something like that. If this is too much for you, you don't have to continue. I can even take you back to Georgia if you want."

But Vanessa shook her head resolutely, her eyes shimmering with determination despite the tears that clouded her vision. "No, I want to stay and help you solve this," she insisted.

I nodded. "Thank you!"

As Vanessa leaned in for a hug, I found myself instinctively wrapping my arms around her, drawing her close. This time, it felt different—more natural, less awkward.

In that fleeting moment, as I held Vanessa close, I realized that forming an emotional bond with her was breaking through my personal space bubble. She is growing on me.

"Okay, here's the plan," I began, pulling back slightly from the hug to look Vanessa in the eyes. "We take the day to recover and start fresh tomorrow on finding Lynette. Today, let's just try to have some fun. We don't know what we're getting into with this."

Vanessa nodded in agreement.

"Stacy was involved in this, and I think she was going to come clean, so someone took her," I continued, the pieces of the puzzle slowly falling into place in my mind. "Maybe someone she's working for. She was always weird when it came to discussing her work."

"We need to be careful," Vanessa interjected, her tone cautious, her eyes scanning our surroundings as if expecting danger to lurk around every corner. "In case someone is following us."

"After we figure out who this woman is, I need you to take this stuff to the cops," I said, my voice serious. "I would, but I'm kind of on the wanted list. They need to see that I was being stalked. And the photo at the restaurant might help the missing person case."

Vanessa's eyes widened in understanding. "Good plan," she replied.

"So, what do you want to do today? You can choose whatever you want," I offered. But as she gave me a hungry look, like a ravenous wolf eyeing a juicy steak, I instantly regretted my words.

"Is there a zip-lining place around here?"

*Hmm! I did not expect that.* "Yeah, there is a really good one, actually," I replied, a smile tugging at the corners of my lips.

She extended her hand to help me up. "Well, what are we waiting for?" she exclaimed.

With a grin stretching from ear to ear, I grabbed her hand, and we made our way to the zip-lining place. The thought of soaring across canyons and feeling the rush of wind against our faces filled me with excitement.

I kept bugging Jordana to come with me, but she was too scared of heights to take the plunge. It wasn't Stacy's thing, either. Vanessa will actually be the first girl to go with me. This girl is pretty badass.

As we arrived at the zip-lining facility, the sight of the tall towers and sturdy cables only heightened my anticipation. The instructors greeted us warmly, their enthusiasm contagious. After a brief safety briefing, we suited up in harnesses and helmets.

Standing at the starting point, I could feel the adrenaline coursing through my veins. I glanced at her, and her eyes sparkled with excitement. I took the leap first, the initial drop exhilarating as I zipped through the air. The sensation of flying through the air is the ultimate feeling of freedom.

As I reached the end of the line and landed safely, I turned to see her zipping down behind me, a wide grin on her face. When she touched down, she slapped my hand in excitement and declared, "That was so freaking awesome. This one is so much better than the one in Georgia."

"Wanna go again?" I asked, a grin spreading across my face as I eagerly anticipated her response.

"Uhhh... yes!" she shouted with excitement.

We hurried back to the start of the zipline, the thrill

of another ride coursing through our veins. This time, we decided to race each other, each of us determined to claim victory. I won, of course... okay, fine... she beat me. Either way, with a fun day like this one, we both won.

After grabbing some mix to make drinks and a few snacks, Vanessa and I headed back to the hotel room. As we mixed our drinks and nibbled on snacks, we found ourselves laughing at the predictably boring movies playing on the screen. The alcohol warmed our spirits, easing the tension of this crazy situation we were in.

While Vanessa was pouring herself another drink, I headed to the bathroom. Of course, I walk by just as she is turning. We collided, my hands instinctively reaching out to steady her and prevent her from spilling her drink.

Our eyes met at that moment, and I could sense she wanted more. Her eyes portrayed she craved more than just a fleeting touch. Why wouldn't she? To her, I am her husband.

As I came out of the bathroom, I noticed traces of tears glistening in her eyes.

*How do I make her feel better?* I had to think about her, to prioritize her well-being over my own tangled emotions. I needed to let go of my feelings for Stacy, at least for a while, and focus on supporting Vanessa, regardless of our marital status.

"You can come over and lay on my bed with me," I suggested nervously.

Vanessa's eyes lit up with excitement at the suggestion. It wasn't even two seconds before she was beside me on the bed. That was quick.

We looked at each other and both smiled. I reached out my arm, offering for her to cuddle with me, and she didn't hesitate to scoot closer, snuggling into my chest. I have to say, as much as it pains me to admit this, something felt right about her in my arms. Or perhaps it's just because I'm a tad tipsy right now.

# Chapter 23

## STACY

### Ten Days Ago

As I stood in front of the mirror, nervously adjusting my outfit for my meet up with Zyler at the park, a knock at the door startled me. Is that him? Did he come here instead? At times like this, I wish my door had a peephole. My heart raced with anticipation as I swung the door open.

Three men stormed into my apartment like they owned the place, my boss leading the pack. Panic surged through me as I struggled to comprehend what was happening. My boss's expression was a storm cloud, dark and foreboding, and his commanding tone brooked no argument as he ordered me to sit in the living room.

I complied, my heart hammering against my ribs.

My boss's voice cut through the silence like a knife. "Stacy, there are no words to describe how I feel right now," he began, his voice dripping with a potent mix of anger and disappointment. He paused, as if gathering his thoughts, before continuing with chilling certainty. "I know you were in my office before you moved. And I know you found some things." His gaze bore into mine like hot coals searing through my defenses. "I was going to let it slide, but now you're on your way to run your mouth to Zyler." He tapped his phone ominously, his eyes flashing with accusation. "I see your messages sent to his phone. I have access to all of his messages."

He shoved his phone in my face, showing the message I had sent Zyler about wanting to talk and not being honest with him. Seeing my message on my boss's phone gave me an incredibly creepy feeling I had never experienced before. A wave of nausea crashed over me like a tsunami, the sickening realization sinking in that my privacy had been violated in the most egregious manner possible. The pulse in my throat pounded like a fresh wound, each beat sending shockwaves of panic through my veins. I struggled to draw breath. My lungs constricted by fear.

My boss leaned in close, his presence suffocating as he invaded my personal space. His breath was hot against my skin as he closed his eyes, inhaling deeply before exhaling with a frustrated sigh. He rubbed his head as if battling with inner turmoil before straightening up and pacing the room with restless energy.

"I liked you, Stacy. You had promise," he admitted, his voice heavy with disappointment. "But now... I have to do something about this."

With a sudden burst of fury, he kicked the coffee table over. The sound of shattering glass echoed through the room like a gunshot. Holy shit! I flinched at the sound.

"I'm sorry," I managed to squeak out. "I won't go meet him, I swear. Just... just let me go."

All three of the men laughed. The scariest one among them, the one with a scar marring his face, nodded no to my boss.

"It's too late. We can't let you go, Stacy. Not now!" he intoned, his voice dripping with menace. "You have two options, come willingly or not. Either way, you are leaving with us."

Panic gripped me as I scrambled to my feet, desperate to escape from them. With a sickening crunch, my foot slipped, and I tumbled to the ground, agony lancing through my hand and knee as broken shards tore into my flesh, leaving behind trails of blood. I cried out in agony, my vision swimming in tears as I struggled to regain my footing. Before I could, strong hands closed around my arms like iron vices, wrenching me back into their clutches. Summoning every ounce of strength, I kicked out wildly, connecting with one of the men and sending him crashing into the kitchen table, the impact scattering its contents across the floor.

But my victory was short-lived as the other men swiftly moved to restrain me. A sickly sweet odor wafted towards me, and before I could comprehend its significance, a cloth was pressed over my nose and mouth, suffocating me into darkness.

# CHAPTER 24

## ZYLER

I woke up to find Vanessa still asleep beside me in my bed. *Crap!* We must have fallen asleep. Wincing with the hope that nothing happened, I carefully extricated myself from the tangled sheets and tiptoed to the bathroom. My mind was already buzzing with thoughts about the day ahead.

As the warm water cascaded over me in the shower, I tried to shake off the unease lingering in the back of my mind. It is a big day; we are heading to Las Vegas to find this Lynette Bolton woman. It is only a couple of hours' drive from here, not too far.

Stepping out of the bathroom, I found Vanessa getting dressed, standing there in red lingerie. I felt a sudden flush of embarrassment flood my cheeks at the unexpected sight, instinctively averting my gaze and stammering out an apology.

Vanessa laughed. "If I was worried about you catching me, I would have waited for the bathroom," she teased, her voice playful.

I chuckled nervously, unsure of how to respond. "I don't know what to say to that," I admitted, a hint of color creeping up my cheeks.

Her flirty grin widened. "Are you blushing?"

I shrugged, trying to play it cool. "The shower was hot," I replied, hoping to divert the attention away from my embarrassment.

"Sure... the shower," she replied in a skeptical tone, amusement dancing in her eyes.

"That's my story and I'm sticking to it," I replied with a grin, trying to maintain a light-hearted tone despite the lingering awkwardness. "Are you just going to stand there with your shirt off or put it on so I can look again?"

"Fine! If I must," she said in an unreadable tone.

"Well, you don't have to, but going out there," I

pointed out the window, "might be a bit awkward, is all."

She laughed and quickly pulled her shirt over her head. "You have a point," she admitted, glancing over at the camera. "Hey, can I see the pics one more time before we head out?"

"Go right ahead," I replied, gesturing toward the camera.

As she scrolled through the photos, she stopped and stared at one. "Holy shit!" she exclaimed, her voice tinged with shock and disbelief.

Alarmed, I hurried over to her. "What is it?"

"This is the day we met." She pointed at the picture and continued, "That's me in the chair."

My eyes widened in surprise. "That's you? Your hair is so..."

"Blonde?" she blurted out, anticipating my response.

"Yeah! I didn't pay attention to that photo because I didn't know who it was."

"I was sitting there waiting for my date. He didn't show. Just as I was about to leave, my chair broke and I fell on the floor. That's when I met..." she hesitated to say more.

I couldn't contain my curiosity. Screw denial! "That's when you met me, isn't it?"

I'm still not convinced it's actually me. Guess I can't bluff my way out of this one with the pictures and DNA evidence, can I? It only hurts her more. I grabbed her hand and plopped down next to her. I told her straight up how I was feeling. I said, "Let's just roll with it."

Her eyes got a little misty as she responded, "Thank you! You're right. It was the day we met. You picked me up off the floor, and we hit it off right away."

"Looks like I picked you up another way too," I teased.

She chuckled. "You said the same thing that day."

I laughed. "You really fell on the floor?"

"Yes, and in front of everyone. It was so embarrassing," Vanessa recalled with a hint of discomfort in her voice.

"I bet it was," I replied sympathetically.

"That was eight years ago," she continued, her expression turning serious. "They have been watching us this whole time."

As Vanessa pondered the unsettling revelation, a knot of dread tightened in my stomach. A chill ran down my spine at the thought. They weren't just watching me; they were watching her too. "Um, Vanessa..."

"What?" she asked, turning to look at me.

"What if your date didn't stand you up? What if... there was no date?" I finally voiced the chilling possibility that had been gnawing at me.

Her eyes widened in realization, mirroring the alarm that churned within me. "You think maybe I was talking to the person taking the photos, and they got me to go there because you were there?"

I nodded, my thoughts spinning with the implications. "I know it seems crazy. But this whole thing is so messed up. I wouldn't be surprised if that's what happened."

Vanessa stood up abruptly, shaking her arms as if to dispel the unsettling thought. "We really need to find this woman."

"I'll say," I agreed, snatching my keys off the dresser. "Here, take the keys and start the truck. I need to use the bathroom. Be right out."

# CHAPTER 25

## VANESSA

### TWO HOURS LATER

As I gradually regained consciousness, my mind swam in a disoriented haze. The darkness surrounding me was suffocating, pressing in on all sides like a heavy blanket. I couldn't move—I was trapped.

Groping blindly in the darkness, my hands made contact with hard, unforgiving metal. I pounded on the surface, my fists connecting with a dull thud. "Let me out! Help!" I shouted.

But there was no response, only the eerie silence of the

trunk engulfing me like a shroud. Fighting back the rising tide of panic, I forced myself to think rationally. I needed to find a way out, and fast. With trembling hands, I explored every inch of the cramped space, searching for any sign of a latch or handle.

My heart raced, pounding in my chest like a jackhammer as I struggled to make sense of my surroundings. What the hell is happening? The last thing I remember was going outside to start the truck.

Suddenly, a muffled sound reached my ears—a distant murmur of voices. My heart skipped a beat as I strained to listen, but the words were indistinct.

Did one just say Zyler? The name sent a shiver down my spine. Desperate now, I pounded on the walls of the trunk, calling out for help with a voice hoarse with fear.

Gasping for air, I struggled to fill my lungs. It felt as if my chest was giving my heart and lungs a bear hug. It must be the people watching him. They took me, but why? What do they want?

I tried to draw in a deep breath, but my chest still felt constricted. Each inhale was a battle, my lungs screaming for oxygen.

We stopped. Oh, no! I hear them... suddenly the trunk

door opened. One of them grabbed the rope tying my hands together and pulled me up. He grabbed me and threw me over his shoulder. I wanted to fight. To kick myself free. But I knew I wouldn't get away. There were two of them, maybe more. I was blindfolded and my hands bound together. The more I fight back, the more it will piss them off. So, for once in my life, I kept my damn mouth shut.

As I was ushered into an isolated room by the men, my heart pounded frantically in my chest. A cocktail of terror swirled within me. The scene that met my eyes intensified my confusion—a room filled with three other people, their faces displaying a mix of fear and curiosity.

As I took in my surroundings, a sense of surrealism washed over me. Without delay, my ankle was secured to a robust post at the room's core, granting me mobility, but absolutely no hope of escape. Strangely, the room exuded a warm and inviting vibe, contrasting sharply with the grim reality of my situation.

To my right, I could see a bathroom, its sterile white tiles offering a stark contrast to the rest of the room's cozy atmosphere. On the left corner, a potted plant added a touch of life to the otherwise sterile environment. What the hell is this place? Who are these people? No one uttered a word.

Along both sides of the room, there were three cells each, small and equipped with a bed. Oddly, they remained unoccupied. That must be where they sleep. I realized with a sinking feeling in my stomach.

I locked eyes with a blonde woman across the room, her face filled with a mix of curiosity and fear. She looks so familiar. Beside her, a black woman stood up and made her way to the bathroom. In the corner by the plant, a young girl with red hair and freckles was completely absorbed in a book. Wonder how long they have been here?

As I took a seat beside the blonde lady, her brown eyes met mine, and a jolt of recognition shot through me. Shit! I think that's Zyler's friend from the pics. I whispered the name, "Stacy," and her eyes widened in acknowledgment. She pressed her finger against her lips, signaling me to remain quiet.

"Are we being watched?" I whispered, barely audible, my heart pounding in my chest. She nodded subtly, her gaze flickering towards the other side of the room.

The black woman joined us. Her eyes scanned the

surroundings as if searching for an escape route for the hundredth time. Why won't they talk? What happens to us if we do? The questions filled my mind as silence enveloped the room, broken only by the soft hum of the ventilation system.

The black lady sat on the recliner chair with a pencil and paper, appearing gripped in drawing a picture. Leaning close to Stacy, I whispered, "I'm Vanessa." She looked at me with a shocked expression, swiftly getting up and hurrying to the bathroom. Oh no! Did I upset her?

She remained in there for quite some time, and the longer she stayed, the more certain I became that I had indeed upset her. Guilt washed over me. I glanced up to see the young girl looking at me, her blue eyes glistening with homesickness.

Stacy emerged from the bathroom and leaned in close to me, her tone carrying a hint of demand rather than suggestion as she whispered, "You should really use the bathroom if you need to." I waited a couple of minutes, trying not to make it obvious, and then began to wander around the room as if I were inspecting it.

Once inside the bathroom, my eyes fell upon a note peeking out from behind the soap. I retrieved it cautiously and read its contents.

> They listen and watch constantly. If we talk about anything other than the room or everyday conversation, they punish us. If we obey, they leave us alone and provide us with food. It's quite good considering the situation. Don't divulge personal details. The only place I have found with no cameras, believe me, I tested, is this bathroom. We communicate in here. When you're done reading this, tear it into the tiniest shreds and flush it. The young girl is Emma, and the other lady's name is Shayla. We believe we're somehow entangled in a conspiracy, and that's why they're keeping us here. It's the only thing that makes sense. My boss is one of them. Remember, we can talk, just nothing personal or about anyone you know. Not sure if you know this, but your husband is still alive.

I already know he's alive. Guess she doesn't realize I was with him looking for her.

Quickly, I tore the note into shreds as instructed and

flushed them down the toilet, ensuring no trace re-mained.

# Chapter 26

## ZYLER

As I entered Las Vegas, the neon lights of the city shimmered in the distance. My thoughts were consumed by worry. It had been four agonizing hours since I last laid eyes on Vanessa. The same individuals who had abducted Stacy must have taken her as well. The journey felt interminable, with tears clouding my vision multiple times. I couldn't shake off the overwhelming sense of guilt and helplessness gnawing at me. I should have just had her wait till I was done. Why did I send her out to start the truck? I'm such an idiot.

Thankfully, Vanessa had *dropped* the keys. I clung to

the hope that it was intentional, a sign that she was okay and not because she had been hurt. She better not be hurt. The mere thought of anything happening to *either* of them was unbearable.

I slapped myself in the face, hoping it would knock some sense into me. Get it together, man. Losing control wouldn't help me find them. It isn't going to help me find Lynette, either. I need to find her now more than ever.

Pulling up to the Salvation Homeless Shelter, which was the address scribbled on the paper by Stacy; I pondered whether this was where Lynette worked or lived. Stepping out of the car, I approached the front door with a mix of apprehension and determination.

Inside, the shelter bustled with activity. People moved about, some chatting quietly, others seeking refuge from the streets. I spotted a worker standing near the entrance and approached her, my eyes scanning the room.

"Excuse me," I began, trying to keep my voice steady. "Is Lynette Bolton here?"

The worker looked up, her expression kind but slightly wary. "Today's her day off," she replied. "But she'll be here tomorrow."

Relief flooded through me. "Thank you," I said, offering a small nod before turning on my heel and heading back to my truck. At least I know Lynette is still alive and hasn't been taken herself.

Next on the list... Lynette's house. Just gotta make a pit stop at a gas station first. I could really use a drink before I do this. But showing up with alcohol on my breath would look even worse.

As I stepped out of the gas station, a woman charged toward me, her footsteps pounding against the pavement as she closed the distance between us. Before I could react, her hand connected with my cheek with such force that my head snapped to the side.

She began to cry, her words tumbling out in a frantic rush. "How dare they let you out of prison after only two years!" she exclaimed, her voice laced with anger and sorrow. "You murderer!"

Confusion washed over me. "What are you talking about?" I managed to choke out, still reeling from the unexpected assault.

She didn't answer. She lunged at me again, her fists clenched in fury. This time, I was prepared. I tried to hold her off, but she raised her knee and rammed it right into my nuts. Pain radiated through my body, and I crumpled to the ground, clutching my groin.

"What the hell, lady?" I gasped, struggling to regain my breath.

She wasn't finished. "I should kill you myself, Blake!" she screamed, her voice raw with emotion.

*Blake?* My mind raced. Who the hell is Blake? I tried to speak, to tell her she had the wrong person, that my name wasn't Blake. But the throbbing pain below left me unable to form coherent words. Before I could gather my wits, she ran off.

Jesus! I thought Las Vegas was supposed to be a fun time.

Limping back to my truck, every step a pain coursed through my body. I struggled to make sense of what had just happened. It took me a minute to gather myself before I could even contemplate driving to Lynette's place. What was that woman talking about? At first, I thought maybe she had seen me on the news regarding Stacy's case, but her mention of two years and Blake threw me off completely. She definitely has the wrong guy! Am I stuck in a freakin' never-ending nightmare or what? About to open my eyes and find myself lying next to Jordana? This can't be real.

Despite the hurricane of emotions inside me, the drive to Lynette's flew by faster than a squirrel on Red Bull. I pulled up out front, staring at the numbers on the house. Gulping down some air, I braced myself to knock on her door, knowing I could potentially be greeted with another slap. But I couldn't let fear paralyze me. I had to find answers, and Lynette might be the only one to answer them. With a final, shaky exhale, I reached out and smacked my knuckles against the door, bracing myself for whatever lay on the other side. *Here goes nothing!*

# Chapter 27

From the corner of my eye, I caught a glimpse of movement behind the curtain, and my heart skipped a beat as a woman peeked through the window. Moments later, she opened the door, but left the screen door closed.

"Can I help you?" she asked, her voice tinged with wariness.

"Lynette?" I inquired, hoping I had the right person.

She nodded, confirming her identity. I took a deep breath, steeling myself for what I had to say. "You don't know me, but I think you have some answers that might help me with a situation I'm in."

Lynette studied me for a moment with a guarded look.

"And you are?"

"Oh, sorry," I quickly replied, realizing I hadn't introduced myself. "My name is Zyler Dixon."

Her demeanor softened slightly, and she immediately unlocked the screen door, inviting me inside. But as she did, I noticed her cautious glance around outside, as if checking for someone watching.

I stepped inside her home, taking in the sight of a very cluttered living room. Lynette appeared to be in her sixties, and as far as I could tell, she was the only one living here.

"Can I get you a drink or anything?" she offered, gesturing towards the kitchen.

"No, I'm okay, thanks," I replied, declining her offer.

Lynette patted a chair, gesturing for me to take a seat. I sat down. How the hell do I start this?

As she sat looking at me, I noticed tears were forming in her eyes. Why is she crying? I thought to myself, feeling slightly weirded out by it.

Clearing my throat, I struggled to find the right words. "I found pictures of a file with your name on it," I began, my voice uncertain. "A file full of pictures of me over multiple years. I came here to see if you know anything about this, or why someone would be following me?"

"I knew you would come looking someday," Lynette said softly, her voice tinged with a hint of sadness. Rising out of her seat, she disappeared into another room, leaving me to wrestle with my mounting anxiety. Fear soured through me, a cold knot forming in the pit of my stomach as I imagined the worst-case scenarios. What if she went to grab a gun and is going to finish me off right here?

I was going gray waiting for her to come back. She walked back in, cradling an album like it was her first-born.

"I have something to show you," she said, her voice shaky with emotion. "You may not like what you see, and I understand if you hate me after this. Just know that there wasn't a day that I didn't think about you."

My heart pounded in my chest as she opened the album, revealing photographs of me through childhood. Some I recognized. Others, however, were distant and hazy, yet undeniably me. Each photo was marked with either a Z or a B. I sat staring at them in disbelief, as if I had just seen a ghost steal my pizza.

Tears streamed down Lynette's cheeks as she spoke.

"This is you and your twin brother, Blake," she cried out. "The reason I hesitated at the door is that I didn't know which one you were, and Blake is in prison for murder. It scares me a bit, and if it was him, I would have sent him away."

I listened in stunned silence, struggling to comprehend the bombshell she had just dropped. "I don't understand," I managed to choke out.

Lynette took a deep breath, looking at the photographs before her. "When I had you and Blake, I was in no condition to support you," she explained, her voice heavy with regret. "So, I made the hardest decision of my life and gave you both up for adoption. The agency promised to give me updates and pictures of each of you, to watch you grow and know you were safe."

A surge of anger and betrayal welled up inside me as her words sank in. "Why did you never reach out to me?" I interjected. "You never even tried."

Lynette's eyes brimmed with tears as she continued. "I know, and I'm sorry," she said. "But you have to understand, part of the agreement was that neither of you were to find out I am your mother."

She went on to describe the agony she felt the day she

had to let us go, the last cuddle with her babies, and the heartbreaking realization that she had made the biggest mistake of her life. "I cried for days," she confessed, her voice breaking. "But there was nothing I could do."

As Lynette sat there sobbing, her tears falling unchecked, she begged me to forgive her one day. Her words hung in the air, heavy with remorse and regret, but I remained distant and numb, unable to find the words to comfort her.

I need to get out of here. I stood up abruptly, looking at the woman before me, who I had just learned was my birth mother, and felt nothing but a hollow emptiness gnawing within me. Clenching my jaw in frustration, I finally managed to speak.

"Which prison is Blake in?" I asked, my voice flat and lacking emotion.

Lynette's tears slowed as she looked up at me. "High Desert State Prison."

I nodded. "What is his last name?"

"Coleman," she whimpered, looking at the ground.

I stormed off to the door without saying anything else. "Zyler!" she shouted. "Listen up. The folks keeping an eye on you are no joke. If they catch wind of you being in the loop about me or Blake, you better believe they'll come for you. They made it clear to me to never dare contact you."

I halted abruptly and whipped around to glare at her. "I've got two friends who are missing because of those bastards. If you know anything else, for the love of God, please tell me."

I saw a fiery motherly instinct burning in her eyes. The determination to sacrifice everything for her sons. "I think I know where your friends are. But first, what are their names?"

"Vanessa and Stacy."

"I don't know who Vanessa is. But Zyler, Stacy, is not to be trusted. She was hired to become your friend. I saw her meet you that day. I saw the black SUV she got out of. She works for them. I will bet my life she was offered money like I was for giving you up."

I lost it. Not too often do I yell, but I couldn't hold it in any longer. "Unbelievable. You actually sold your own children? What were we worth?" I snarled, clenching my teeth in anger.

"Let's not do this."

"No, we are doing this. How much were your children

worth, MOM?" I growled.

"A million dollars," she mumbled.

I rubbed my forehead with my hand. I don't think I have ever felt this pissed off in my entire life. "I've heard enough. Where are my friends?"

She quickly provided the location, her tone filled with urgency as she warned me to be careful. "Don't just show up there, or they might kill you... or me," she cautioned.

I didn't even let her finish before I turned and walked out the door. Climbing into my truck, I couldn't shake the sense of betrayal and anger swirling inside me. I wrestled with conflicting emotions, torn between anger at Stacy for manipulating and lying to me, and frustration with myself for falling for her scam.

One thought burned deep in my mind: there was only one person who could feel the pain of Lynette's betrayal as deeply as I do—my so-called brother. Time for his ass to have a visitor.

# Chapter 28

As I walked into the prison visiting area, my heart was racing like I had just stolen a cop car. I was about to meet my long-lost twin brother for the first time, a guy I never had a clue about until now. The guard was like my wingman, leading me through the drill until suddenly I was standing right in front of Blake.

He looked exactly like me, but with longer hair and a rougher appearance. Our eyes met, and for a few moments, we just stared at each other.

Finally, breaking the silence, he said, "I can't believe you're here."

I nodded, struggling to find the right words. "I can't either. I never knew I had a twin until now. Did you know about our lovely mother giving us up for adoption?"

He looked at me, his expression tense with emotion. "Yeah, I found out," he admitted, his voice betraying a hint of bitterness. "It was like a punch in the gut, realizing that our own mother could just... give us away like that."

I nodded, understanding the pain and confusion.

His gaze hardened as he continued, "I went to find you, Zyler. I found you, but I was arrested before I could get to you."

I looked at him, debating on whether to ask him the million-dollar question. *Screw it!* "Did you really kill someone?"

He scoffed. "Hell no. I didn't kill that man. I helped the guy. Next thing I know, I'm arrested for his murder."

My heart sank at his words, a surge of anger rising within me at the injustice of it all. "That's terrible," I exclaimed, my voice tinged with frustration. "How could they accuse you of something you didn't do?"

He shrugged. "Seems like I've always been dealt a bad hand," he muttered bitterly. "But I swear, I didn't do it. Someone framed my ass. I've been trying to clear my name, but... it's not easy from in here."

"They must have evidence that you did the crime. Otherwise, your arrest makes no sense," I insisted, trying to make sense of this chaos.

Blake scoffed again, his voice rising with frustration. "Does any of this make any fucking sense? Something is going on. Something big. And our so-called mother knows more than she's letting on. Don't trust anyone, Zyler."

"Except you, right?" I challenged.

He glared at me, eyes blazing with intensity. "That's up to you. I swear on my life, I did not lay a hand on that man. To be honest, I think someone was keeping me from getting to you."

A torrent of thoughts raced through my mind. People thinking I'm a missing man. The blood in Stacy's apartment. Vanessa vanishing. A brother I never knew about.

I put my hand up to the glass that separated us. Call it twin intuition, losing my sanity, or just trying to hope for something good, but I believed Blake was telling the truth. I think he was targeted before I was. "I believe you."

He let out a deep sigh of relief. "You don't know how good it feels to hear someone say that."

Considering I would have given anything for Vanessa to say she believed me, I had a good idea of how it felt.

Blake leaned forward, his voice low and urgent. "Listen, there's a warehouse I found out about before my arrest. It's about three hours—"

Before he could finish, I cut in. "I know exactly where you're talking about. Lynette told me where it is."

Blake's expression twisted in disbelief. "That bitch," he growled, his voice laced with anger. "She sent me away without telling me. If she would have told me, I could have done something about it before I got sent to prison."

I looked at him, my own shock mirrored in his eyes. "I think she realized hiding is over. We both know what she did. If she wants any forgiveness, she has to act like a mother and put us first for once."

A bitter laugh escaped Blake's lips. "That woman will never be my mother," he declared.

I nodded in agreement. "I hear you there."

Before we could continue, the guard interrupted, announcing that visiting time was over. As they began to escort Blake away, he turned to me, a fierce determination burning in his eyes. "Take them down, my brother," he urged.

"They have people I care about. They are going down. Hang tight. I'm going to get you out of here or die trying."

As I watched them lead Blake away, a sense of realization washed over me. I had a brother—a brother in prison who I knew without a doubt was innocent. I just needed to find a way to prove it.

Determined, I gathered all the evidence I had managed to compile—the camera with the photos, Lynette's address, the warehouse location, and a letter detailing everything I knew about the disappearances of Stacy, Vanessa, and myself. With shaking hands, I sealed the envelope.

Arriving at the police station, I handed the envelope to the lady behind the desk, urgency evident in my voice as I pleaded, "Please, have the officers look at this as soon as possible. Lives may be at stake."

She nodded solemnly, taking the envelope from me with a reassuring smile. "I'll make sure they get it right away."

Leaving the station, my heart pounded with anxiety.

Time was slipping through my fingers, and I couldn't afford to waste a single second. Determined to uncover the truth and bring justice, I drove straight to the warehouse.

As I approached, the sight of guards patrolling the area confirmed my worst suspicions. Ducking behind a nearby building, I carefully scanned the surroundings, plotting my next move.

Suddenly, a black man approached me from the shadows, swiftly covering my mouth before I could react. My heart leaped in my chest as I stared at him, my eyes wide with fear. He leaned in close, his voice a whisper. "Shhh..."

# CHAPTER 29

## VANESSA

As I slowly blinked my eyes open, the harsh reality of my surroundings flooded back—a cold, dimly lit cell with rusted bars and the faint sound of distant footsteps echoing through the building. My heart sank as I realized it wasn't a dream. I was really here, trapped in this nightmare. How the hell am I going to get out of here?

As if sensing my despair, Stacy, who was in the cell across from me, caught my eye and motioned with her eyes toward the cell beside mine. I furrowed my brow in confusion, unsure of what she meant. I looked to see who was in the cell, but I could only see a gray cement wall.

I shrugged my shoulders in response, not understanding her silent message.

Stacy greeted me with a soft "good morning," and I returned the sentiment, my voice strained with worry. Suddenly, a man's voice from the cell beside me blurted out, "Vanessa?" My blood ran cold as I recognized the voice. *Zyler!* Oh, no! They got him too.

Before I could react, a figure emerged from the shadows and approached Zyler's cell, their stern expression a clear indication of authority. "No names!" they reprimanded, their voice cold and unyielding. Panic coursed through me as they began to pull Zyler away.

"Zyler," I wanted to scream out, to tell him I was here, but fear held me back. I couldn't risk them coming for me next. The desperation in his eyes was a reflection of my own, tears welling up as he fought against his captors, reaching out toward me.

"Vanessa," he shouted, his voice cracking with emotion. His anguish was palpable, each syllable a dagger to my heart.

My heart shattered as I watched him being dragged away, his final words echoing in the silence of the cell. "I love you, Vanessa."

"Stop!" the captor barked, yanking Zyler away with brutal force. I watched helplessly, my own tears blurring the sight of his struggle.

I turned to Stacy, tears streaming down my face, and saw her crying too. It hit me then—she must love Zyler. Hearing him declare his love for me must have been like a stab to her heart. The realization added another layer of pain to the already overwhelming despair.

But amidst the turmoil, a glimmer of hope flickered within me. Hearing Zyler say those words, it felt like he finally remembered me. That connection, no matter how fragile, was a lifeline in this sea of darkness.

A guard approached, unlocking our cells with mechanical efficiency. Stacy wasted no time. She bolted for the bathroom. As she emerged, her expression was solemn, her eyes reflecting a mix of determination and sorrow. She leaned in close and whispered, "Your turn."

I nodded, my heart pounding as I made my way to the bathroom. Once inside, I splashed cold water on my face, in an attempt to reduce the puffiness of my eyes. As I scanned the small room, my eyes fell upon a note tucked into a secret hiding spot. With trembling hands, I unfolded it, my breath catching in my throat as I read

Stacy's words:

> **We all have had our moments being taken. He will be back. Don't say any names. Don't look like you are waiting for him. Just go on with our normal day, read, draw, etc. When he comes back into the room, use all of your strength and pretend that he is just another person you don't know. Or you will be taken, and let's just say it isn't a pleasant experience.**

I stood there, my mind reeling with the weight of Stacy's warning. Could I really pretend not to know Zyler? The thought of ignoring him, of denying our connection, felt like a betrayal in itself, but I knew that my survival depended on it.

Taking a deep breath, I tore the letter into pieces and flushed it down the toilet, erasing any evidence of our exchange. Each shred swirling away felt like a piece of my heart being torn apart, but it was necessary. I had to protect Zyler, Stacy, and myself.

Rejoining Stacy in the shared area, I forced myself to adopt a façade of calm indifference, burying my emotions deep inside. Every muscle in my body ached with the effort of pretending. Pretend, Vanessa. Pretend you don't know him.

I made my way to the couch and took a seat, trying to appear as casual as possible despite the turmoil raging inside me. My hands trembled slightly, and I clasped them together to steady them. Stay strong.

Emma dashed past me, heading for the bathroom next, followed closely by Shayla.

We hadn't been sitting for long when someone entered the room carrying plates of food. The tantalizing aroma filled the air, making my stomach churn with hunger. I wished I had the appetite to enjoy it, but the weight of our situation pressed heavily upon me.

Still, I knew I couldn't afford to pass up the opportunity to eat. Who knew when the next meal would come, or if it would come at all? With a heavy heart and a queasy stomach, I forced myself to take a bite, each swallow a reminder of the uncertainty of our fate. The food tasted like ash in my mouth, a bitter reminder of our captivity.

A guard barged into the room, his presence looming over us like a dark cloud. He grabbed my arm and led me to the door. Stacy's defiant shouts filled the air. "She didn't do anything."

Shayla joined in. "Leave her alone," she demanded, her voice trembling with anger and fear.

I attempted to wrench myself free from the guard's iron grip, but it was useless. His hold only tightened, his fingers digging into my skin like steel claws, leaving bruises in their wake. Pain shot through my arm.

In that moment, a chilling realization washed over me—I had to cooperate if I wanted to survive. Fighting against him would only lead to more pain, more suffering. With a heavy sigh of resignation, I steeled myself and allowed the guard to lead me away.

I stumbled forward as the guard pushed me into a dark room. The door slammed shut behind me, leaving me in darkness. I winced as my elbow collided with the unforgiving floor, a sharp pang of pain shot through me.

"Who is there?" a voice called out from the corner of the room, the sound of desperation and fear lacing his words.

"Zyler," I whispered, relief flooding me as I recognized his voice. I hurried toward him, my hands fumbling to remove the blindfold that obscured his sight.

"Vanessa," Zyler cried out, as I removed the blindfold.

"Yes, it's me," I said, tears welling up in my eyes as I

took in Zyler's appearance. He looked different from the other day—rougher, wearier—but to me, he was still the love of my life.

Zyler reached out and touched my face, his fingers tracing my features as if he couldn't believe I was real. "Hey beautiful," he moaned softly.

My heart swelled at his words, a warmth spreading through my body. "Hey handsome," I whispered back.

Without hesitation, Zyler pulled me into his arms, his embrace a lifeline in the suffocating wickedness. I nestled against his chest, seeking solace in his warmth, feeling a rush of relief wash over me.

Our lips met in a fervent kiss, a silent exchange of all the love and longing that had consumed us in our time apart. It was a kiss born of desperation and fueled by the fiery passion of our shared ordeal.

As we reluctantly broke apart, breathless and clinging to each other, a memory surged to the forefront of my mind. "Did you find the keys I threw under the truck?" I blurted out.

Zyler's brows furrowed in confusion. "What keys?"

"The keys I threw under your truck when they took me," I clarified urgently. "Did you find them?"

He appeared confused. "When?"

"The other day when I went out to start the truck," I said in a frustrated tone.

A tear traced a path down Zyler's cheek, his voice trembling with emotion. "Babe, I haven't seen you in years. The last thing I remember is getting us Chinese food and being chased off the road by a black SUV. Then I woke up here."

I struggled to process his words. A flood of relief mingled with disbelief washing over me. "You remember me?"

"Of course I do. You are my wife."

I fought to contain the torrent of emotions threatening to overwhelm me. But the floodgates burst open, tears streaming down my face uncontrollably. I collapsed to my knees, the weight of everything crashing down on me. Zyler knelt beside me, wrapping his arms around me in a futile attempt to soothe my anguish.

As my husband held me close, my mind raced with a singular, terrifying question. Who the hell did I spend the last week with? Was it just a dream?

# CHAPTER 30

## ZYLER

I struggled against the pressure of the man's hand cover-ing my mouth, desperate to make noise, to alert some-one, anyone.

"My sister is in there," he explained. "Do you have someone in there, too?"

I nodded vigorously, my heart pounding with fear and anticipation.

"The name is Marcus. We need to figure out a plan to get inside," Marcus whispered, his breath hot against my ear. "I'm going to remove my hand. Don't make any noise."

I nodded again, my throat constricted with tension.

"Who are you?" Marcus asked.

"Zyler. My friends are in there," I whispered back, my voice trembling with adrenaline.

"Take this," Marcus instructed, pressing something cold and solid into my palm. I looked down to see a handgun resting in my hand, my fingers instinctively curling around it.

"Whoa!" I gasped. I never used a gun in my life. "I don't know how to..."

"The safety is on. Just flip it off, point, and squeeze the trigger if needed," Marcus interrupted, his tone urgent and authoritative.

I stared at him like a deer caught in headlights.

He glared at me, his eyes flashing with impatience. "Have any better ideas, man?" he snapped.

I swallowed hard, my throat dry with anxiety. "What if I kill someone? I can't shoot someone," I stammered, my voice trembling with doubt.

"Okay! Just let them kill you instead. Is that better?" Marcus retorted.

"Well, no. But..."

"Listen, man, I'd really love to debate self-defense right

now, but I need to save my sister. So, listen up," Marcus interrupted, his voice stern and determined. "I'm going to distract them, like I have the wrong place, and you sneak to the back and find a way in. There's no one at the back. I checked."

"Why do I have to be the one that goes in?" I protested weakly.

"You are killing me smalls," Marcus groaned. "Man up and grow some balls."

We are dead. This is a terrible plan.

Marcus headed to the front, distracting the guards. With a surge of adrenaline, I snuck in through the back window. The sudden wail of sirens pierced the air. Thank God the cops are here. There was no one in sight, but the ominous steel door on the left sent shivers down my body. As I approached it cautiously, the sound of footsteps echoed down the hall, sending a wave of fear through me. With trembling hands, I pushed open the door and shut it quietly behind me, holding my breath.

"Zyler," a voice whispered, making me jump in the air. I spun around to see Vanessa standing there, her eyes wide with relief. Beside her stood a man who looked exactly like me.

"Vanessa," I blurted, rushing over to her. "Are you okay?" I looked at the man beside her, my heart racing with confusion and disbelief. "Blake?"

Vanessa leaped into my arms, clinging to me with palpable relief. "I'm so glad you're okay," she murmured. As she stepped back, her eyes darted in shock to the man standing next to her, then returned to me with a bewildered expression. Tentatively, she placed a hand on his shoulder. "This is my husband, Zyler... I think?"

I looked at him, a whirlwind of emotions churning inside me. We stared at each other in disbelief. "Your name isn't Blake?"

"No. My name is Zyler Dixon. Who are you? And who is Blake?"

"I'm Zyler Dixon. Blake is my..." I paused, the truth hitting me like a ton of bricks. "Twin brother, apparently." I laughed. *He is messing with me.* "It's okay, if you were using my name, Blake. You can fess up."

Vanessa looked at me. She pointed at me, then at her husband, her mouth opening and closing as if searching for the right words. "Umm..."

"I don't know what you are talking about. I'm not pretending to be anyone," he responded.

"We have to hurry. The police are outside," I blurted out.

We listened intently by the door. The other Zyler took the lead, guiding us through the hallway. "Over here, you two. We have to get the others."

"Stacy is here," Vanessa whispered.

"I figured," I responded grimly.

Following Zyler, we reached another room. He swung the door open, revealing three faces— a black woman, a red-headed kid, and Stacy.

"Zyler!" Stacy's voice rang out, filled with relief as she ran up to hug me. "I'm so glad you're safe."

I gently but firmly backed her off. "I'm glad you're okay, too. I hope I was worth the money," I uttered, my words heavy with bitterness.

Tears welled up in Stacy's eyes as she looked down, struggling to meet my gaze. "I was going to tell you that day, I swear," she pleaded.

"I know. Doesn't change anything. I cared about you, Stace..." My voice faltered as a tear escaped my eye. "I was in love with you."

"You meant a lot..." Stacy began, but I cut her off.

"Don't. I was nothing but a paycheck to you," I declared, my heartache etched across my face.

Turning to the black woman beside her, I asked, "Do you have a brother named Marcus?"

Her eyes widened in surprise. "Yes, is he okay?"

I nodded towards the front entrance. "He's outside."

"He came for me?" she asked.

"Yes. We better get out of here. Follow me, everyone," I commanded.

Peeking out the door, I scanned the area. There was no one in sight. Motioning for the others to follow, we sprinted down the corridor towards the room I had entered through. Suddenly, a gunshot echoed from outside. Shayla's panicked scream pierced the air.

I grabbed her shoulders, trying to steady her trembling form. "Marcus has a gun. It might have been him, or the cops. I'm sure he's fine," I reassured her, my own heart racing with fear.

Raising the gun in my hand, I added, "This is his, too."

Pointing towards the window, I directed Vanessa, Zyler, Shayla, and the kid to crawl out one by one. As they made their escape, I heard footsteps approaching down the hall. Turning back, I found myself face to face with a man aiming a gun at me.

Before I could react, Stacy's voice rang out, warning me to get out of the way. With a shove, she pushed me to the side, taking the bullet meant for me. My heart stopped as she collapsed to the ground, groaning in pain.

Instinctively, I aimed the gun at the assailant and fired. The man crumpled to the floor. Shock and horror washed over me as I realized what I had done. Oh my god! I killed him.

I looked down at Stacy. "No, no... Stace. Hang on." I kneeled beside her, trying to hold pressure on her wound. My eyes widened at the sight. So much blood. I'm going to be sick. I held my throat tight. Now is not the time. I could feel her blood gushing around my hand. This is not good. "Stacy, hang on. The cops are here. Hang on a few minutes."

Her grip tightened on my hand. "Zyler, it wasn't about the money. I swear on my life, the money meant nothing after I got to know you. I tried to get out of it, but they threatened me."

I swallowed hard. "It's okay, we can talk about this later," I replied, trying not to cry.

She shook her head. "I love you, Zyler. I love you more than I loved anyone. I was going to tell you..."

But then her words trailed off, and panic seized my heart as I realized something was wrong. "Stacy?" I shook her gently. "Stace, wake up." But there was no response. "No! You can't die on me," I pleaded, tears streaming down my face as I sobbed into her chest. "No... no..."

I got up and walked over to the prick I shot. Kicking him repeatedly, I screamed at him, "What did you do?" I turned his face to see the man that killed the woman I love. A wave of recognition hit me in the gut. Shit! That's the guy Vanessa was seeing. Mr. Runaway! I couldn't hold it in any longer. I threw up beside him. I just killed Vanessa's ex.

In a flurry of motion, the warehouse doors burst open. Cops swarmed in.  I raised my hands in surrender, my voice hoarse as I called out, "This woman needs help. That man shot her and tried to shoot me. So, I shot him."

They led me out of the building. I saw Shayla, Marcus, the kid, Vanessa, and the other Zyler standing outside. Relief flooded through me as I stumbled towards them, tears welling in my eyes.

"You're safe," I uttered through choked sobs.

Vanessa's voice cut through the air, her concern evident as she asked about Stacy. I couldn't bear to look her in the eye as I shook my head, the tears flowing freely down my cheeks.

"Someone shot her. She didn't..." I faltered, unable to find the strength to finish the sentence.

"I'm so sorry," Vanessa said, leaning in to hug me.

I pulled back from her and held her arms. "There is more. The guy that shot her was..."

"Was?" she questioned.

"Warren," I responded. "He was one of them. I think I..." I took a deep breath. "Killed him."

Vanessa's expression was inscrutable, a mix of emotions flickering across her features. "I would have too," she agreed, her voice catching in her throat as tears welled in her eyes. "Stacy was a good person. She didn't deserve to..." she started sobbing.

Our conversation was interrupted by a woman's voice calling out a name. Turning, I saw a red-headed couple pushing through the crowd, tears streaming down their faces as they wrapped their arms around their daughter.

# CHAPTER 31

## TWO WEEKS LATER

Standing by Stacy's grave, Vanessa and I shared a moment of quiet reflection.

"You and I had a connection," Vanessa murmured, her eyes locked on the gravestone in front of us.

"We did," I agreed, wrapping my arm around her shoulder and pulling her close. The warmth of her body was a comfort amidst the cold reality of our loss.

"But it wasn't genuine," I continued, my voice steady but tinged with sadness. "Your feelings for me were because you thought I was your husband. And I got close to you because of the situation. I started to doubt my memories, wondering if you were actually my wife."

My gaze drifted toward the other Zyler, who stood solemnly by a nearby tree, lost in his own thoughts. The resemblance between us was uncanny, and it was easy to see how Vanessa had been mistaken.

"My heart was always with..." I trailed off, my voice catching in my throat as I struggled to finish the sentence. The memories of Stacy, her laughter, her strength, flooded my mind.

Vanessa's gaze dropped to the ground. "With Stacy, I know. She really loved you, Zyler. I could tell."

I closed my eyes, letting the pain and love wash over me. "I know," I whispered, my voice barely audible. "She died for me. She proved her true feelings." Tears welled up in my eyes, cascading down my cheeks. "I just wish we could have had a life together," I admitted, my voice trembling.

I locked eyes with Vanessa. She squeezed my hand, offering silent support. "What do we do now?" she asked.

I smiled gently. "We're going to walk over to your husband. You're going to give him the biggest hug and start your life together again." A thought crossed my mind, making me chuckle. "And... don't mention the little hotel strip show."

Vanessa laughed, a light sound that felt like a small break in the clouds. "Deal. What about you?"

"Well," I said, thinking of the future, "I'm going to start over. Might even change my name." I grinned. "Get to know my brother. Sounds like Blake is being released tomorrow."

"Still can't believe the guy he supposedly killed was actually alive. Who would have thought?" Vanessa added, shaking her head.

"He hid well those two years. I'll give him that," I scoffed. "Blake and I are gonna stay together for a while until we can figure out where to go next."

"Sounds like a good plan," she replied. As we walked toward Zyler, Vanessa asked, "What would you change your name to?"

"Considering I just rose up from the worst time in my entire life, I think Phoenix seems fitting."

"Phoenix Dixon. I like that. It suits you."

I shook Vanessa's husband's hand. "Take care of our girl," I said, followed by a chuckle.

"Of course. Don't be a stranger. It would be nice to get to know you," Zyler replied, pulling Vanessa closer to him.

"I will swing by from time to time. I know where you live," I joked, winking at Vanessa.

With a final wave, I turned and headed toward my truck. I took a deep breath, feeling the cool morning air fill my lungs.  As I passed the grave, I whispered a silent promise to Stacy. I would live for both of us, carrying her memory with me as I faced whatever came next.

# CHAPTER 32

## THREE MONTHS LATER

Over the past three months, I have learned a great deal.

At the heart of this scheme was Lynette Bolton, a woman who thought she was carrying twins but was unknowingly pregnant with identical triplets—three boys born into a world of manipulation and deceit. The mastermind behind this plot was a doctor affiliated with a shadowy organization, one that had been quietly monitoring and selecting cases for years at a hospital in Nevada. Lynette's pregnancy presented a rare opportunity for a twisted experiment, one the organization was willing to pay any price to pursue.

Lynette, in a vulnerable state, was approached by representatives of this organization. They offered her a staggering sum of one million dollars to give up her 'twin' sons for adoption, promising they would be placed in loving homes. Desperate and overwhelmed, Lynette agreed, unaware of the full extent of the conspiracy. She had no idea that one of her sons was being kept hidden from her, a secret even she was not privy to.

The organization's plan was diabolical in its simplicity. Two of the triplets were adopted out under the condition that they would grow up with the same name, while the third would bear a different name. This wasn't a mere act of cruelty, but a carefully constructed experiment designed to probe the depths of familial intuition and identity.

I was manipulated into moving to the same household as Vanessa, the wife of the 'hidden' triplet. I looked exactly like her husband, shared his name, and even had a similar voice. Vanessa, unaware of her husband's identical brother, couldn't fathom the possibility that I wasn't him—even as my personality and laugh differed from his.

As the layers of deception unraveled, I found myself doubting my own memories and identity. The pictures of a man that looked exactly like me, the neighbors recognizing me, and the DNA match began to erode my sense of self, instilling a form of brainwashing. The organization had crafted an elaborate ruse, planting clues and manipulating circumstances to make me believe I was someone else entirely.

To remove Blake from the picture, they framed him for the murder of one of their employees, ensuring he was imprisoned and out of the way. This action not only protected their secret but also isolated me further, leaving me more vulnerable to their manipulation.

Meanwhile, my other brother, the 'hidden' triplet whose identity remained a secret to all but a select few within the organization, had to go 'missing' for a period of time. His absence was a crucial component of the organization's plan, creating the illusion of a seamless transition as I moved into the house to assume the role of Vanessa's long-lost husband. This deception was designed to test the limits of human identity and the power of soulmate recognition.

Vanessa, struggling with the sudden return of her husband and the subtle differences she couldn't quite place, was caught in a whirlwind of confusion and emotion. The organization watched from the shadows, meticulously recording our interactions and the strain on our relationship. Each moment of doubt and every whispered question was data for their twisted experiment.

As I lived under the guise of being Vanessa's husband, I experienced a growing sense of disorientation. The more I tried to reconcile my memories with my new reality, the more my sense of self frayed at the edges.

The realtor, unsuspecting of the true nature of the house's history, was merely a pawn in the organization's conspiracy. She was informed that she was selling an estate house, shown a falsified death certificate in Vanessa's name, and led to believe that everything was legitimate. Her role was crucial but unknowing, as she facilitated the final piece of the organization's intricate plan.

Unbeknownst to Vanessa, her boyfriend—a key player in the corrupt organization—played a pivotal role in coordinating the deception. He arranged to be on 'dates' with her during the showings, ensuring that she remained unaware of her house being sold. On the day I moved into the house, he conveniently took her out of town, ensuring she was none the wiser. His unexpected visit at the door that day was likely a check-in, to see if I stayed or bolted after seeing Vanessa.

I still have nightmares about the killing. Nightmares of being a serial killer, of going to hell. I don't regret it, though.

People often say that we meet our soulmates in strange ways, but mine being paid to befriend me and manipulate me to move to Georgia pretty much takes the cake. In the wake of her betrayal, anger and mistrust clouded my thoughts. But in those last moments, I saw a glimpse of her true feelings for me. There was a flicker of genuine love in her eyes. In her own way, she was a victim too. And tragically, she didn't survive, leaving me to mourn the future I could have had with her.

Though the pain of losing her may never fully heal, I cling to the silver linings that came out of all of this. The void that had lingered within me for as long as I could remember was finally filled. As a triplet, I had always sensed that something was missing, an indescribable emptiness that haunted me even amid relationships and friendships. It was as though a piece of myself had been lost. But with the arrival of my two brothers, everything changed. There is a sense of belonging that washed over us. We share a bond I never knew existed.

For the first time in my life, I felt truly complete. With my brothers by my side, I no longer felt alone in the world. The bond we shared was a powerful antidote to the years of manipulation and deceit we had endured.

My amazing sister-in-law, Vanessa, is unlike anyone I have ever met. Her unwavering loyalty had turned her from a hostage in my home to a hostage in my heart. Despite our initial friction, she grew on me, claiming a space that would forever be hers. And let's just say, I'm so thankful we never gave in to our urges that night in the hotel. Family get-togethers will be awkward enough.

In the aftermath of this tragedy, so many things came to light. One of them being the truth about my parents. It turns out they were paid off to change their last name and make my name Zyler Ray Dixon. This revelation was a bitter pill to swallow, but it gave me clarity. I legally changed my name to Phoenix Zyler Dixon. I'm still debating on whether I should change my last name.

Emma was abducted to study the differences between a mother and a father reacting to the same trauma and the impact a missing child could have on a marriage. Some pretty twisted shit, if you ask me. The inhumanity of it all is shocking, knowing that there are people capable of such cold, calculated cruelty.

Shayla reunited with her family after a year of captivity. Her brother Marcus had fallen victim to this corrupt organization years prior, at the age of 18, along with five other teens who had gone missing on the same day. But that is a story for another time.

# EPILOGUE

## PHOENIX

### EIGHT MONTHS LATER

I swung the door open and barged past Zyler and Vanessa, heading straight for my beautiful little niece. Holding her in my arms, I felt a surge of emotion. I hadn't realized how attached I could get to such a small human. Grinning, I looked at my brother and said, "Yup. Just what I thought, she takes after her uncle."

Blake added, "Everyone knows she takes after me most."

They all laughed. "That's because you both look exactly like her father," Vanessa joked.

"Hey now, don't steal my thunder. Stacy is my little buddy. I'll try to pencil you guys into the schedule now and then." Vanessa snatched her from my arms. "Hey, I wasn't done holding her."

She looked at me with a smirk. "Well, unless you plan to hold her while I feed her..."

"Nope! I'm good," I interrupted, raising my hands in surrender. "That's my brother's territory."

"Blake has an awesome new girlfriend," I announced, changing the subject.

Blake waved his hand dismissively. "Yeah, yeah, she's alright."

I frowned. "Alright? Amara is more than just alright. She's sweet, caring, and really supportive of Blake."

Vanessa smiled warmly. "That's great news, Blake! I'm glad you found someone."

Blake grunted noncommittally, his attention already drifting back to his phone.

Turning to me, Vanessa tilted her head. "Is there someone special in your life?"

My smile faltered slightly. "Uh, not really. I mean, Blake has been trying to get me back into the dating scene, but I'm just not ready yet."

Zyler shook his head. "I don't blame him," he said quietly. "If anything happened to Vanessa," he paused, his arm instinctively wrapping around her, "I wouldn't be able to look at another woman for years." Zyler jumped up to grab something. "This reminds me, something came for you in the mail. Not sure who it's from," Zyler said, handing me a postcard from Montana.

"What's this?" I said, examining the postcard. There was something written on it and a small pouch taped to the back. I carefully removed the pouch and unfolded the postcard.

Phoenix,

I heard about one of the Morgans. She is doing well. Hopefully soon she will be reunited with the other. Here is a little gift. Take care of yourself.

Seanna

With a trembling hand, I opened the pouch and pulled out a key. A storage shed key. Vanessa and I exchanged a glance. A big smile crept across our faces. No way! How? Without hesitation, I pocketed the key. "Looks like I'm taking a road trip to Montana."

# <u>The End</u>

# About the Author

Jessica was born in the heart of South Carolina. She experienced an unique childhood, with a few tragedies that shaped her perspective and fueled her creative spirit.

After her father's untimely passing, and her mother's subsequent remarriage, she moved to Canada as a young child. Amidst the constant flux, her unwavering passion for writing and storytelling emerged as a stable companion, providing stability throughout the years.

She is a mother of four boys. Due to circumstances, she

was unable to return to work outside of the home after the birth of her twins. Sparking her interest to become an author.

Dive into more of her gripping tales with "Echoes Of The Hunted" and "A Stranger Within." Don't miss out on these captivating reads!

# ALSO BY

JESSICA LYNN SORENSEN

Secrets linger like shadows in Joplin, Missouri, where the sins of *infidelity* have a deadly consequence. When a serial killer terrorizes the town, preying on those who break their vows, one woman manages to escape, aiding in the *capture* of this ruthless killer. But when new threats start appearing and her abusive ex resurfaces from the dead, Angela's world spirals into a web of deceit.

Continue to the next page for a preview.

# Echoes Of The Hunted

## Prologue

Serial killers are a lot like readers if you think about it.

Readers choose books based on a variety of factors, whether it be the gripping cover, intriguing synopsis, or simply the feeling of the moment. They crave a variety of thrills, whether it be the gradual build-up of tension, shocking turns of events, or heart-pounding, adrenaline-fueled action.

In the same way, serial killers select their prey, taking into account various factors such as appearance, personality, familiarity, or even their own current state of mind. Their motives vary, from deriving sick pleasure in their victim's suffering, seeking revenge, to finding enjoyment in the act of taking a life.

Hell, murder can be so *addicting* that even readers themselves crave more of it. I bet you can't disagree with that. If you did, you would have DNF'd this after the first line. Well, well, seems like you and I are more alike than you thought.

As for me, my killings serve a different purpose. I eliminate those who pose a *threat* to the person I idolize. I can't let anything ever happen to them. That is why, at this exact moment, a woman has to die.

It's *exhausting* really. I had no intentions of killing today. However, this lady just had to go *witness* my idol disposing of a body. I can't let her flap her mouth to the cops about it. Judging by the look she had on her face, that is exactly what she plans to do. I can't risk that. I'm their *biggest* fan. I serve to *protect* them.

So, here I am.

I smothered her face with chloroform until she fell limp, then hoisted her over my shoulder. Plunging through trees in this dreadful darkness, searching for the perfect spot to bury her. *Why is she here in the woods alone at night, anyway?* Luckily, I have the necessary materials stashed in my trunk to deter cadaver dogs from detecting her. A crucial step to avoid getting caught is to always be prepared.

I'm not a gruesome killer. I'm not going to cut her all up, rip her to shreds, or make her beg for mercy. I don't even *want* to kill this girl. I grew up with my dad saying, "Son, never lay a hand on a woman or child." For the most part, I *obey* that. But in this case, I have to kill her because she had the audacity to be in the wrong place at the wrong time. I could bury her alive. Then technically, it wouldn't be by my hand; it would be the lack of oxygen killing her. The thing is, I don't want this poor woman to suffer. That's why I'm going to dig her grave, throw her in it, hop down there, and slit her throat while she's unconscious.

No suffering! Painless!

You see, I do have mercy. I'm not a monster. You are probably wondering why I am waiting to do her in. Why risk her waking before I get a chance to do it? Common sense, really. I don't want blood smeared all over the ground. Good way to get caught. I'm not an idiot. It is better my way. After I'm finished, I'll spread a bunch of leaves and branches over the top to make it blend in. No one will ever know Mia Crosby is hibernating underneath their feet.

ALL I WILL SAY IS... DON'T MESS WITH THE GAME CHANGER.

# A Stranger Within

What would you do, if you woke up in an abandoned shed without the memory of *who* or *where* you are? Drugged, starving, hurt... BUT... you are free to go. *Nothing* is holding you there. Going into the darkness outside, all you have is a gimped leg, ripped clothes, and not a *clue* what to do.

This is Cassidy Miller's reality. A reality that just might be *better* than her actual life. It is an *odd* situation when the mind can't handle certain things - so instead, *it hits the reset button*. It's like being born all over again, learning things for the first time.

With the help of a man she befriends named Caleb, can she piece her identity together? Is Caleb really who he says he is? *Day By Day* - Her heart is growing feelings – Her mind is growing suspicion.

CONTINUE TO THE NEXT PAGE FOR A PRE-VIEW.

# A Stranger Within

## Part Of Chapter One

I slowly blinked my eyes open. The world came into focus in shades of darkness.

*Burr!* I could feel the biting cold seeping into my bones. I attempted to sit up, but my body felt heavy. Like I had been sleeping for days.

*Where the hell am I? How did I get here?*

The building was old, and its walls were peeling. The air was thick and full of dust, and every sound I made echoed. My mind raced to grasp any semblance of memory.

*Who am I?*

I couldn't even remember the appearance of my face.

My legs trembled beneath me as I stood up. The floor under my feet creaked with each step. It felt as if the very walls were closing in on me.

*Suffocating me.*

Ouch! I grabbed my head with my hands. It seemed as though my head was being squashed in a vice.

Cautiously, I placed one foot in front of the other, trying to avoid the floor sections that sounded like they might give way at any moment. I extended my hand, allowing it to glide along the rough, cool surface of the walls, seeking any clue about the purpose of this forsaken place. However, the building remained silent.

My mind raced with questions I couldn't answer.

*Where am I at?*

*Is it dangerous to go outside?*

My entire body hurt. The pain was intense. Burning in areas that I didn't even know existed.

The door burst open with a bang, causing me to jump in the air.

*Holy shit!*

As if I needed another thing to be scared about. All I could grasp was my weakness, the gnawing hunger, and how drugged I felt. You'd think I had been run over by a truck.

Stepping outside, I scanned the path ahead.

*Great! I can't see a damn thing.*

A cool breeze whispered through the trees, stirring the leaves into a gentle rustle. Each step sent a sharp twinge through my knee. I winced, biting down a groan.

The wind caused the trees to cast eerie shadows across my path, making the vibe even creepier. Every rustle, every snap of a twig underfoot, heightened my awareness of the potential danger lurking in the darkness.

"Well, this is just awesome," I muttered to myself. "Don't mind me. I'm just walking down a mysterious road in the middle of nowhere, with a screwed-up knee, and no idea where I'm going. Typical day over here." I laughed, realizing I sounded like a crazy person talking to myself.

As I strolled along the path, I could hear something howling in the distance.

*What the hell was that?*

My heart raced. I attempted to run, but my knee was not making it easy. I felt exposed to the wild creatures lurking around, stalking my every move with unseen eyes.

The howls grew louder.

"Come on, trees," I shouted. "Don't you have a mirror around here? I could really use a reminder of what I look like before I die!" The absurdity of my comment provided a brief distraction.

I finally reached a highway. The distant lights of passing vehicles provided a glimmer of hope. I stood there... my torn clothes flapping in the wind. My scruffy appearance was likely to freak out any passing driver. I couldn't help but smile, imagining what I'd say if someone were to stop.

"Hey there, kind stranger," I chuckled to myself. "I need a ride. You want to know where? I haven't quite figured that one out yet. My name? It's right on the tip of my tongue. Why am I out here wandering around alone, like a psycho? I wish I had an answer to that. The truth is, I have no fucking clue."

The more I tried to stop, the more my thoughts poured out of my mouth.

Extremely dry mouth.

What is that awful taste in my mouth?

You'd think I was chewing on metal.

With each passing car, my hope flickered and then waned as it continued by me.

*Finally! A decent person in this world.*

A vehicle actually slowed down. The truck's brake lights lit up the dark. A man rolled down the window. His eyes flickered with curiosity.

"Thank you for stopping," I murmured, the words feeling inadequate for the overwhelming sense of relief that flooded through me. "I appreciate it."

He nodded. "You don't look like you're doing too well. What happened?"

I swallowed hard. The dryness of my throat hindered my ability to speak for a moment. "All I remember is waking up in a creepy abandoned shed. No idea who I am, or how I got there. It's all a bit of a blur, to be honest."

Completely aware that I was providing way too much information to a stranger—details that could make bad intentions far too easy. I had no other choice.

"We better get you to a hospital. They can check you over and they might have a record of you there. I'm Caleb, by the way," he added, reaching out to shake my hand.

"Nice to meet you, Caleb. I'd tell you my name, but..."

"It's okay, hop in," he beckoned, gesturing toward the passenger side with his head. I slid into the seat and shut the door. He grinned at me, then joked, "I'll be expecting a postcard when it comes back to you."